To What End the Sabbath?

An Exegetical Study

To What End the Sabbath?

An Exegetical Study

Amar Pandey

2018

To What End the Sabbath? *An Exegetical Study*–published by the Rev. Dr. Ashish Amos of the Indian Society for Promoting Christian Knowledge (ISPCK), Post Box 1585, Kashmere Gate, Delhi-110006.

Online order: http://ispck.org.in/book.php

Also available on amazon.in

ISBN: 978-81-8465-670-1

Laser typeset by

ISPCK, Post Box 1585, 1654, Madarsa Road, Kashmere Gate, Delhi-110006 • *Tel:* 23866323

e-mail: ashish@ispck.org.in • ella@ispck.org.in
website: www.ispck.org.in

To
Dr. David Hymes
and
Mrs. Anna Hymes

Contents

Foreword

The invitation to offer the foreword for this important book on the Sabbath was welcomed with great delight. As noted in the Preface, this book had its origin in the thesis work that Amar did under my direction at the South Asia Institute of Advanced Christian Studies in pursuit of his M.Th. degree. Over the course of the many months of research and writing, Amar and I enjoyed hours of reflective discussions on the purpose of the Sabbath as rooted in the biblical teaching. His decision to pursue this course of study was informed by two specific concerns of his pastor-teacher's heart.

The first of these concerns was pastoral in nature. This is captured by his observation, "In the twenty-first century when people are involved in the 'rat race' of achieving more and more, and accumulating more and more, the call to rest is urgent" (106, in the section labeled "Periodic Rest"). As a pastor, Amar is rightly troubled that Believers today—including many overworked ministers—are not applying the Sabbath principle as expressed particularly in the Old Testament and are experiencing burn-out and fatigue that rob them of the joy of *resting* in the Lord's provision and sufficiency.

The second of these concerns is pedagogical in nature. This is captured by his observation, "Christianity today wrongly emphasizes corporate worship or church attendance based on the Sabbath without the mention of rest from labor" (16, conclusion to chapter 1). In the second chapter of this work, Amar lays out his strong argument that the primary concern of the Sabbath regulations focused on the need for rest (giving urgency to his pastoral observations), not on the need to gather for worship. So his teacher's heart seeks herein *not* to suggest that worship on the Sabbath is unwarranted *but* rather to correct the misunderstanding that worship alone was sufficient for fulfilling the Sabbath principle.

While this work was undertaken in order to meet an academic requirement, it is infused with pastoral and pedagogical insight that all Believers—especially those in his home region of South Asia—need to incorporate into their lives. May this work be used by the Lord to help facilitate a better balance in the work-rest cycle of Believers until we enter by God's grace into that Eternal Rest (Heb. 4:9) anticipated in the Divine Rest of Genesis 2:2-3.

Steven W. Guest, PhD
Educational Consultant and Professor of Old Testament
South Asia Institute of Advanced Christian Studies
Bangalore, India

Preface

This book is primarily an exegetical study of the Sabbath in the Old Testament. Nevertheless, chapter 1 provides a brief historical survey of the Sabbath practice among God's chosen people from pre-exilic times to the period of Rabbinic Judaism, together with the major theories on the origin of the OT Sabbath. In addition, the beginning of the synagogues and their impact on later Judaism and subsequently on Christianity is also discussed.

Chapter 2 deals with the key OT passages related to the weekly Sabbath regulations and expressions. Chapter 3 deals with the sabbatical and the Jubilee years, which are extensions of the Sabbath law. Since the book is primarily concerned with the weekly Sabbath, this chapter will be relatively brief. Moreover, the Sabbath day is hotly debated among Christians today; no one really debates whether or not Christians should observe sabbatical and Jubilee years.

Chapter 4 will look at the New Testament's witness to the Sabbath, particularly that of Jesus and Paul. Because the book's focus is on the Sabbath in the OT, the study of the NT will be brief. The chapter will then discuss how Christians can be informed by the Sabbath in light of our study thitherto, i.e., the manner in which the church/Christians can apply the OT

Sabbath regulations, taking into consideration the Christ event and NT teaching.

The study focusses on the final form of the texts. This book is a mildly revised version of the thesis entitled "To What End the Sabbath?: An Exegetical Study of Key Biblical Texts" submitted at South Asia Institute of Advanced Christian Studies for the degree of Master of Theology. Although not the modern norm, the first letter of the pronouns referring to the persons of the Trinity has been capitalized.

I am truly grateful to Dr. Steven Guest for his assistance, able guidance, and for writing the Foreword. I also wish to thank ISPCK for publishing this work. I am forever grateful to God for my wife Sarita and for our children Sujhav and Kritagyata. Big thanks to my parents Dr. Dilip and Mrs. Meena, and to my siblings Pranaya and Rebecca and their families.

Soli Deo Gloria!
Amar Pandey (Chhetri)

Abbreviations

Books and Bible Versions

BDB	*Brown-Driver-Briggs Hebrew and English Lexicon: With an Appendix Containing the Biblical Aramaic* (1906); Rpt. by Hendrickson Publishers
ESV	English Standard Version
IBHS	*An Introduction to Biblical Hebrew Syntax* by Waltke and O'Connor (1990)
KJV	King James Version
NASB	New American Standard Bible
NET	New English Translation
NICNT	New International Commentary on the New Testament
NIV	New International Version
NIVAC	NIV Application Commentary
NJB	The New Jerusalem Bible
NKJV	New King James Version
NLT	New Living Translation
NRSV	New Revised Standard Version

OTG	Old Testament Guides
TNK	JPS Tanakh
TWOT	*Theological Wordbook of the Old Testament* (1980)
WBC	Word Biblical Commentary
WHS	*William's Hebrew Syntax*, 3d ed. (2007)

Canonical, Deuterocanonical, and Pseudepigraphical Books

Gen.	Genesis
Exod.	Exodus
Lev.	Leviticus
Num.	Numbers
Deut.	Deuteronomy
Judg.	Judges
Sam.	Samuel
Kgs	Kings
Chron.	Chronicles
Neh.	Nehemiah
Ps.	Psalm
Isa.	Isaiah
Jer.	Jeremiah
Ezek.	Ezekiel
Hos.	Hosea
Mt.	Matthew
Rom.	Romans

Cor.	Corinthians
Gal.	Galatians
Col.	Colossians
Heb.	Hebrews
Pet.	Peter
Jud.	Judith
Macc.	Maccabees
Jub.	Jubilee

General

ANE	ancient Near East
BCE	before Common Era
CD	Damascus Document
CE	Common Era
J	Yahwist source
MT	Masoretic Text
NT	New Testament
OT	Old Testament
P	Priestly source
PhD	Doctor of Philosophy
SDA	Seventh-day Adventist
STP	Second Temple Period

Introduction

The Sabbath is the most reiterated command in the Bible (see Davis 6). Moreover, this command is part of the Decalogue that Christians generally take as normative even though they consider many other OT commandments obsolete, e.g., animal sacrifices, dietary laws, etc. The Sabbath commandment is also the longest in the Decalogue. In addition, its central position in the Decalogue has been widely accepted.[1] However, for Christians, this commandment is probably the most obscure among the ten. Douma writes, "No commandment has occasioned as much controversy surrounding its interpretation as this fourth commandment" (109).[2] Bass says that the commandment is "in some ways the most puzzling" (28-29).

Multiple issues are debated concerning the Sabbath. Is Sabbath a creation ordinance or only a part of the Mosaic Law? Is Sabbath observance mandatory for Christians (or all human beings) or is it simply Jewish? If it is mandatory for Christians, then should it be observed on the seventh day or the first day? How should it be observed? The study of the Sabbath generally revolves around these questions (see Appendix 1). The discussions are ongoing and no consensus has been reached in any of the questions posited. However, in this study we will attempt to go a little deeper into the issue of what was the primary concern of the Sabbath, especially of the weekly Sabbath. The reason for this is that it has been generally assumed in biblical scholarship that the concern of the Sabbath day in particular was "rest and worship," while some scholars observe that the Sabbath did not involve worship. On the one hand, "rest and worship" mentioned in the same breath as the requirement of the day is commonplace; on the other hand, a few voices claim that only rest was required of the ordinary Israelites (more below). The former is usually mentioned without defense because it is a widely held belief and the latter is stated briefly while commenting on Sabbath passages; but as far as I am aware no substantial work has been done either to evaluate the assumption or to show that the Sabbath involved rest alone. Hence, this study is essential and important because it attempts to investigate that very issue, namely, the Sabbath's primary concern—rest and worship or rest alone—by scrutinizing key biblical texts on the subject.

The study is also warranted because the Sabbath was deemed so important that its violation was understood as a cause of the exile (Ezek. 22:8, 26, 31; Neh. 13:17-18). Christians today generally believe that they keep the Sabbath through church attendance or corporate worship, yet many are unaware of the primary concern informing the Sabbath regulations. We will study the Sabbath day, the sabbatical year, and the year of Jubilee because these three are foundational for our understanding of the OT Sabbath. Thus, the question that this study attempts to deal with is this: What is the primary concern informing the Sabbath regulations and their expressions in the OT?

In *Sabbath and Synagogue: The Question of Sabbath Worship in Ancient Judaism*, McKay surveys the Sabbath from the OT times to the second century CE and finds no evidence of worship on the day for non-priestly Israelites; rather it was the day of rest. She surveys the Hebrew Bible, the NT, Apocrypha and Deutero-canonical literature, writings of Philo and Josephus, the Greco-Roman writers, etc., but finds no reference to worship even in the synagogues. Synagogues, she says, were centers for learning the word rather than for worship.[3] Her conclusion might be misleading because of her definition of worship (see 3-4, 14, 248; "From Evidence" 186), which is quite narrow.[4] However, what concerns us here is chapter one of her book (11-42)[5]—the study on the OT—and the conclusion she reaches is that there is no reference to "worship" in all of the OT for ordinary Israelites; only the priests were involved in rituals at the temple. The only reference to ordinary Israelites' worship on the Sabbath, according to McKay, is found in eschatological texts. If McKay is correct, then the Sabbath is primarily a humanitarian law. Harrelson seems to agree: "It is the absence of religious duties to be performed on the Sabbath that makes the day so striking" (84). Bosman concurs that for the Israelites the Sabbath involved abstaining from work without any specific cultic activity prescribed for the day. The priests did work on the Sabbath which required sacrifices in addition to those offered on other days (Num. 28-29); but there is no indication of the general populace being involved in any cultus. Citing Ezek. 46:1, 9, Bosman nonetheless adds that there seems to have been some communal assembly in the temple in the *postexilic* times (1159-60). However, OT scholars in general take for granted that worship was part of the Sabbath.

Dressler is a case in point. He maintains that the Sabbath was to be "one day in seven in which they could *worship* God and refresh their bodies" (27, emphasis mine). Moreover, in concluding his article, he states, "Consequently, the Sabbath should have been celebrated as a day of joyfully *assembling before God*" (35, emphasis mine). These words suggest that the Sabbath was to be the day of communal worship. Moreover, McCann notes that there is no sign of cultus on the Sabbath in the early premonarchic period but he repeatedly states that in the monarchic period and thereafter the day involved cultic observance/activity/celebration (in addition to cessation from work) (249-50). To this can be added Waterman's views. Citing Lev. 23:1-3 in particular, Waterman states, "This can only mean that it was regarded as a day for the *calling together of the congregation of Israel to worship. In the early history* of the Israelites, the sabbath was a day of welcome rest from labor and of *solemn worship at the sanctuary of God*" (184, emphases mine). Jastrow contended long ago that the Hebrew Sabbath has a Babylonian background and was initially a day of propitiation of deity with atoning characteristics, i.e., it was a day for cultus. It was a day of rest for the deity, not for humans. Sabbath as the day of rest for human beings is a later development in Israelite religion (312-52). On the contrary, Olson states, "*In its earliest stages* of development in ancient Israel, the sabbath, scholars believe, was *simply a day of rest from work without any association with worship*" (50, emphases mine).

Miller, in the third chapter of his *The Ten Commandments*, says that there are two aspects to the Sabbath commandment in the Decalogue, namely, service of the Lord and resting. He believes that keeping the Sabbath and ceasing from work on the seventh day were likely distinct observances originally that were later combined together into one commandment. For Miller, ceasing from work is only a part of sanctifying the day; the Sabbath was always meant to provide time for worship (117f). Similarly, Packer contends that the spiritual (e.g., worship) takes precedence over the physical (e.g., recreation) on the Sabbath; the rest from work provides opportunity for serving the Lord. Drawing from Matthew Henry he says that the Sabbath provided 'holy rest' so that there could be 'holy work' (66-68). Ross also mentions that the Sabbath made room for "physical refreshment"; but he speaks of the day primarily in terms such as "worship," "spiritual service," "spiritual rest," "holy assembly," and "service to the Lord" (396-406). On the contrary, Block notes that the weekly Sabbath in the OT did not involve communal worship activity (e.g., assembly) for the Israelite community; rather it was a day to take rest and be refreshed (*For the Glory* 272f).[6]

The argument of this book is that the fundamental principle of the Sabbath law in the OT is that every person should be treated with dignity. Having been created in His image, everyone has "worth" in the eyes of the Creator. The Sabbath law covered all of God's people—from rich to poor, and from master to slave; it even covered household animals. The Sabbath regulations and their expressions in the OT seek the welfare of each individual. The Sabbath day's concern is that everyone gets rest one day out of seven, including the most vulnerable, viz., the slaves and even the household animals. In addition to the rest/Sabbath for the land, the sabbatical and the Jubilee years' concern is to prevent the poor from being endlessly exploited as the regulations for these years include cancellation of debts, release of slaves, and return of the land to the original owner. The cultic aspect of the law, if any, is secondary—the law being primarily humanitarian. Our study will investigate the key OT texts on the Sabbath regulations and their expressions. The study will then briefly look at how the church/Christians today should respond to the OT Sabbath regulations in light of the Christ-event and the NT teaching.

Before we proceed, it is necessary for us to understand what we mean by "worship." Varieties of definition of worship are available. McKay defines worship as "a purposive activity, whereby people of similar beliefs assemble to carry out similar rites and rituals in order to pay homage, with adoration and awe, to a particular, named deity" ("From Evidence" 186; see also *Sabbath and Synagogue* 3-4, 14, 248). Block describes worship in these words: "True worship involves reverential human acts of submission and homage before the divine Sovereign in response to his gracious revelation of himself and in accord with his will" (*For the Glory* 23). Allen and Borror write, "*Worship is an active response to God whereby we declare His worth*" (16, italics in the original; see Hill xviii-xx for few more definitions of worship). However, as Hill notes, defining worship is not an easy endeavor because worship is "both an attitude and an act." Likewise, it is both "a concept as well as a relationship" (Hill xviii). We will thus not attempt to define worship but simply note that in light of the fact that this study deals with legal and festal issues in the OT, for our purposes in this book, any cultic activity (e.g., sacrifices) or communal religious activity (e.g., sacred assemblies) qualifies as worship.

Endnotes

[1] For example, it is commonly held that this commandment builds a bridge between the first part of the Decalogue containing commandments with relation to God and the second part containing commandments with relation to one's "neighbors."

[2] Some, like Roman Catholics and Lutherans, take the Sabbath commandment to be the third. However, in this work, we will consider it the fourth commandment.

[3] See especially chapters 1 and 9. Shorter and earlier versions of her findings in this book are found in her "New Moon or Sabbath?" and "Evidence to Edifice: Four Fallacies about the Sabbath."

[4] Beckwith too finds her definition of worship "excessively narrow" (*Calendar and Chronology* 25 n. 16).

[5] See also McKay, "From Evidence to Edifice" 186-87.

[6] See Appendix 1 for further literature review on issues related to the Sabbath.

Chapter 1

Sabbath from its Origin to the Period of Rabbinic Judaism

Historical studies of the Sabbath in the early OT times are in short supply. The likely reason is that the Hebrew Bible is probably *the* source that sheds light on the Sabbath practices of YHWH's people at the time. The discipline of source criticism has made it difficult to sketch such history because the biblical texts have been highly fragmented with the result that the texts on the Sabbath are generally considered P material, hence late—exilic and postexilic.[1] The commands and expressions of the Sabbath from the pre-exilic period recorded in the Bible are considered later interpolations. However, the results of source criticism, and the documentary hypothesis in particular, have been questioned by scholars in recent decades; and there are multiple versions even among the adherents.[2] As mentioned earlier, we will look at the biblical texts in their final form. This is not to deny that there were sources which the biblical writers drew from or that there have been redactions over centuries before the OT received its form as we have it today.

In this chapter, we will briefly look at the Sabbath observance by the people of Israel from the earliest OT times to the period of Rabbinic Judaism. But before we do that, we will briefly discuss the origin of the institution of Sabbath.

Origin of the Sabbath

Various theories have been put forward concerning the origin of the institution of Sabbath and there is no consensus among scholars. The theories begin with the idea that the Sabbath could not be Israel's own creation and should have its precedent(s) somewhere outside of the Israelites. Let us look at the dominant theories.

Lunar Origin[3]

The similarity of the Akkadian word *shabattu* (or *shapattu*) with the Hebrew *shabbath* is at the root of lunar origin theories. The connection seemed to be obvious by the discovery of a cuneiform text where the Sabbath day (*umu shabattu*) is considered "a day of rest for the heart" (*um nuh libbi*). Since *shabattu* refers to the full moon day—so they say—some scholars hold that the Sabbath was originally a monthly observance which was later developed into a weekly one. However, there has been no satisfactory explanation as to how and when this change occurred. Moreover, the view that the Sabbath was the full moon day is held primarily because of the occasional juxtaposition of the Sabbath with the new moon in the Scripture (e.g., Isa. 1:13), but Gaster has contended that 'new moon and Sabbath' might well be a merism covering all "sacred occasions." If this is correct, then the Sabbath as opposed to the new moon has nothing to do with the moon (Gaster 264-65). Milgrom holds that the expression חֹדֶשׁ וְשַׁבָּת is not referring to "new moon and full moon" but "it is simply a progression from the less

frequent holiday to the more frequent holiday" as is the case in
חַגָּה חָדְשָׁה וְשַׁבַּתָּה (Hos. 2:11[13][4]); in fact, he is quite emphatic:
"Hebrew *šabbāt*, however, is not and never was the full moon"
(Milgrom, *Leviticus 23-27*, 1960). In addition, the etymological
relationship between *shabattu* and Hebrew *shabbath* has been
questioned (e.g., Hasel 850; O. Hicks 27-30; Haag 389).

In another version of the lunar origin, the Sabbath is
believed to have originated in the taboo days based on the
moon-phases. The theory is influenced by a cuneiform text
discovered in 1869 by George Smith which is interpreted in
terms of the four phases of the moon. The taboo/evil days
(*ume lemnuti*) in the calendar, however, are 7th, 14th, 19th, 21st,
and 28th, which do not fit into weekly cycle as the Sabbath
does.[5] The lunar origin theories share a common problem:
the seven-day cycle is not in sync with the moon phases. The
Sabbath defies any astral movements.[6]

Kenite-Saturn Origin[7]

The theory holds that the ancient Kenites observed the day of
Saturn as a taboo day and refrained from lighting their smelting
kilns. Furthermore, it is held that the Kenites were smiths of
the desert. The Sabbath day is an adaptation of this Kenite
taboo day in which the Israelites were banned from kindling
fire even for household use. Exod. 35:3 and Num. 15:32-36
are cited to support the theory because the passages deal with
the prohibition of kindling a fire on the Sabbath. The theory is
that Moses, the law-giver of Israel, came into contact with the
Kenites through marriage when he fled to Midian (cf. Exod.
18; Judg. 4:11). The underlying assumption is that the Kenites
followed a seven-day week with a day dedicated to Saturn.
Moreover, סִכּוּת and כִּיּוּן in Amos 5:26 are often considered

to be the references to Saturn—the former assumed to be another name for Saturn and the latter a star of Saturn.[8] From this developed the idea that the Kenites worshiped Saturn as a deity. The problem with this theory is that it is based on too many "ifs"; the theory is highly speculative without solid evidence(s). McCann writes, "Unfortunately, this ingenious theory rests entirely upon circumstantial evidence and must be considered little more than pure speculation" (248).[9]

Socioeconomic Origin[10]

Some scholars see the origin of the Sabbath in the market days at regular intervals common in the ancient societies. For example, every eighth day was a market day in Rome. The regular agricultural work ceased on market days, and those days were probably accompanied by social and religious activities. The theory then is that the Sabbath likely was a derivation not from one particular people but from a practice widely prevalent in ancient societies. The problem with the theory is that a pattern of every seventh day as a market day is unattested in the ANE or elsewhere (Hasel 851). Moreover, there is no satisfactory explanation for how a market day transitioned into a no-work-of-any-kind day.[11]

Calendric Origin[12]

Some scholars have suggested the origin of the Sabbath in the supposed existence of the pentecontad (fifty day period) calendar, which was supposedly a common forerunner of the Semitic calendars. In this schema, the year is believed to have been divided into seven periods of fifty days each (a pentecontad). Each pentecontad was comprised of seven weeks of seven days each, and the fiftieth day was a day of festivity.

The year was further comprised of two festivals of seven day periods each, and one was the New Year's Day. The following is a mathematical presentation of this calendric system:

A pentecontad: (7 x 7 days) + 1 festive day = 50 days

A year: 7 pentecontads (7 x 50 days) + (2 x 7 festive days) + 1 New Year's Day = 365 days

As meticulous as the theory looks, the difficulty is that there is no concrete evidence for the existence of any pentecontad calendar (see McCann 248; Robinson, *Origin* 14).[13]

All the theories above have at least one common problem, i.e., they are hypotheses with negligible or no concrete evidence. No satisfactory explanation has been found yet for the extra-Israelite origin of the Sabbath. Hasel puts it well:

> In spite of the extensive efforts of more than a century of study into extra-Israelite sabbath origins, it is still shrouded in mystery. No hypothesis whether astrological, menological, sociological, etymological, or cultic commands the respect of a scholarly consensus. Each hypothesis or combination of hypotheses has insurmountable problems. The quest for the origin of the sabbath outside of the OT cannot be pronounced to have been successful (851).

Moore, in fact, believes that searching for forerunners of the Sabbath among non-Israelites is "irrelevant" (2-3: 21). Recent scholarship, thus, has been focusing more on the biblical texts rather than on the extrabiblical sources for the study of the origin of the Sabbath (so also Bacchiocchi, "Remembering" 74). Many scholars today are inclined to believe that the Sabbath is a unique Israelite creation (see O. Hicks 27-31; Hartley 376; Milgrom, *Leviticus 23-27*, 1960; Zerubavel 17, 18; Harrelson 79-80; Dressler 23; Sarna 111-12).

Israelite Origin

The Bible suggests that the Sabbath originated with the people of Israel by the decree of YHWH. Many theories have been developed concerning the origin of the Sabbath—major ones of which we have just considered—not least because the scholars dismiss a priori that it could have originated in Israel. Meek is a representative: "The origin of the Sabbath is certainly not to be found with the Hebrews themselves" (201). Is this a right stance? Is it impossible that something could have originated with the Israelites? Dressler raises a similar concern (see 23). In the absence of any evidence against it, I believe it is safe to conclude that the Sabbath probably originated with YHWH's chosen people. The OT holds that the Sabbath began at least at Sinai with the giving of the law through Moses. Some sort of observance seems to have been practiced even prior to it (see Exod. 16). The Exodus version of the Decalogue (Exod. 20) connects the institution of the Sabbath with God's ceasing from His act of creation on the seventh day after six days of work in Gen. 1-2. However, the human (or Israelite) observance of the Sabbath seems to have originated following the deliverance of the Israelites from Egypt.

Whatever its origin, our main concern in this study is the Sabbath as espoused by the Bible, the OT in particular. Let us now briefly look at the history of the Sabbath observance from the early OT times to the period of Rabbinic Judaism.

Sabbath in the Pre-exilic Period

The pre-exilic witnesses to the Sabbath observance by the Israelites, as mentioned above, come from the Hebrew Scripture. The earliest recorded Sabbath observance by the Israelites is found in Exod. 16:22-30 on their way out from Egypt toward

Sinai (ultimately Canaan). The only requirement for the observance of the Sabbath here is that the Israelites do not come out of their houses in order to gather manna because no manna will be provided on the seventh day as it is the Sabbath. Verses 23 and 30 specifically say that the day entailed rest or cessation of work. Exod. 23:12 explicitly mentions the only requirement of the Sabbath, i.e., to rest (נוח) "so that your ox and your donkey may rest and the son of your female slave and the alien may be refreshed" (my translation). All other texts dealing with commands with respect to the Sabbath in the Torah mention rest or cessation of work as the requisite of the day (e.g., Exod. 20:8-11, 31:12-17, 35:2-3; Deut. 5:12-15). Num. 15:32-36 talks about a person gathering sticks on the Sabbath day who was stoned to death by the community of Israel at YHWH's command. The man had violated the Sabbath and it involved working on the day. The sole requirement on the Sabbath for ordinary Israelites was abstention from work; no other requirement is mentioned (or observed). Nowhere does the Torah command the Israelites to observe any cultic ritual save the priests (see Num. 28:9-10; cf. Lev. 24:5-8) or to hold corporate assembly (see chapter 2).

Among the pre-exilic prophets, Amos gives a picture of the Sabbath of the time. Amos condemns those that yearned for the Sabbath to be over so that they could attend to their regular business (8:5). The implication here is that work—in this case merchandising—was prohibited on the Sabbath day. Visiting a prophet is seen to be legitimate (2 Kgs 4:23). In a special circumstance, Priest Jehoiada undertakes a coup on the Sabbath against Athaliah to make Joash king (2 Kgs 11:4f; 2 Chr. 23:1f). Jer. 17:19-27, however, unambiguously shows that the Sabbath was to be kept holy by not doing any work on it (vv. 21-22, 24, 27). Texts like Hos. 2:11[13] and Isa. 1:13 are taken by some to say that the Sabbath involved cult and assemblies in the monarchic period (e.g., McCann 249), but the conclusion is not that simple as we shall see in chapter 2.

Thus, the Sabbath in the pre-exilic period clearly had one requirement for the general populace beginning in the pre-Sinaitic times in Exod. 16 to the monarchic period; and that requirement is to refrain from work. The common belief in biblical scholarship that the Sabbath always was the day of rest *and worship* seems unwarranted (cf. McKay, *Sabbath and Synagogue* 11). The belief appears to be a projection back into the earlier period of the practice that developed later in the religion of YHWH's people, particularly the development in the Judaism of the STP (more below).

Sabbath in the Exilic and Postexilic Periods

A major crisis in the life and religion of the Israelites was the fall of Jerusalem in 586 BCE at the hands of the Babylonians. Israelite religion had been highly centralized and revolved around the temple by the Judean kings. The fall of the temple, together with the deportation of the people to the foreign land, meant that there was no place for their religious (i.e., ritual) observance. The laws concerning the Sabbath, circumcision, and kosher diet gained heightened importance in the exile because they did not require a temple, the priest(s), or the Levite(s) (see Anderson 143; Murphy 79, 89; Scott 126). These three—Sabbath, circumcision, and dietary laws—became the prominent markers of the Jewish religion in the exilic and postexilic periods and are instrumental in the preservation of the people and their religion to this day.

Another major historical development in the STP is the establishment of the synagogues. The synagogues are important to our discussion because with their establishment, the Sabbath observance took a new form not envisioned by the Torah. The time of the origin of the synagogues is uncertain. Many scholars believe that they originated in the exilic period in Babylonia due to the absence of the temple worship. Although this is logical and quite plausible, no evidence has been found to date of their existence at the time. Millgram, for example, gives a plausible scenario of how the synagogues could have begun in the exile first through informal gatherings of the Jewish people of a locale at a priest or a Levite's house during the Sabbaths and other religious festivals (cf. 2 Kgs 4:23). These in turn took more formal shape over a period of time, which eventually gave birth to the synagogues (Millgram 63-67; see also Moore 1: 283-84). However, the following words from Millgram suggest the degree of the plausibility of this hypothesis:

> The origin of the house of prayer, later known as the synagogue, is recorded neither in the Bible nor in the postbiblical records. Only *scattered hints* can be discovered in the vast rabbinic literature. But these *vague hints* enable us to make some *plausible conjectures.* The *most logical* of these is that the synagogue had its origin in spontaneous informal gatherings among the Jewish exiles in Babylonia. With a *little imagination* we can reconstruct the situation and clearly see how this remarkable new religious institution was born (64, emphases mine).

Statements in Ezekiel such as YHWH being a sanctuary to His people in their places of exile (11:16) and the elders of Israel coming and sitting before Ezekiel (14:1) are cited as evidence for the existence of the synagogues in the exile (see Scott 139). Moreover, the proceedings of the assembly in Jerusalem convened by Ezra in Neh. 8:1-10, which are similar to that of the later synagogue services, are also put forward as evidence.

These facts are helpful but are very ambiguous to provide any strong proof for the existence of the synagogues in the exile. Hence, we cannot be sure that the synagogues began as early as the Babylonian exilic period. The earliest attestations to the synagogues are in the third century BCE (c. 246-221) from Upper Egypt (see Cohen 111; Scott 139; Smith 259; Filson 78). These institutions could well have begun in the Hellenistic period (so Cohen 107). In any case, there is a general consensus that the synagogues did not exist in the pre-exilic period. With the establishment of synagogues in the STP, worship (prayer and study of the Scripture) became an essential part of the Sabbath (see Block, *For the Glory* 277; Blomberg, "Sabbath as Fulfilled," *Perspectives* 307) which has survived even today.[14] Worship was an essential part of the Sabbath among the Qumran community. For instance, they had thirteen songs meant for the Sabbaths of the first three solar-calendar months and the community believed that in singing these Sabbath Songs, they joined the angels in praising God (see Wassen 505-08; cf. Van Henten 51). For ordinary Israelites, however, *proseuchai*/synagogues mark the beginnings of public assembling for weekly worship.

The postexilic situation reflected in Nehemiah's time shows that the restriction on work continued to be the crucial element of the Sabbath observance (Neh. 10:31, 13:15-21). The "no work" requirement of the Sabbath is found also in the apocryphal and pseudepigraphical literature of the STP. For example, 1 Macc. 2:29-38 mentions some Jews who were willing to die, refusing to defend themselves on the Sabbath day so that they would not desecrate the Sabbath. On the other hand, some adjustments were made during the period by the Jews when it threatened life. For instance, Mattathias and company, after hearing about the death of the Jews who refused to defend themselves on the Sabbath, decided to defend themselves if the enemy attacked them on the day (1 Macc. 2:39-41).

The restriction of work on the Sabbath took ridiculous measures among some groups in the STP. For instance, Scott notes concerning the Essenes: "Their Sabbath practice even prohibited building a fire or emptying their bowels" (216). The latter one is quite alarming. Moreover, Jubilees prohibited even sexual intercourse between husband and wife (Jub. 50:8). Rowland believes that the Jubilees too could have originated with the sect(s) akin to the Essenes (45). The sole "work" that was acceptable on the Sabbath according to the Jubilees and the Damascus Document is offering sacrifices to God; in fact, CD clearly (Jubilees is not very clear) places restrictions even in the sacrifices offered on the day, i.e., only the sacrifice/offering prescribed for the Sabbath is to be brought (Jub. 50:10-11; CD 11:17-18). Of course, eating what was prepared on the sixth day was permitted (Jub. 50:9-10; CD 10:22). In fact, to enjoy feasting seems to be an essential part of the Sabbath (see Jub. 2:21, 31; cf. Jud. 8:6).[15] The Damascus Document allows travel on the Sabbath only up to 1000 cubits (CD 10:21; cf. Acts 1:12) but 2000 cubits was permitted for pasturing (CD 11:5-6). Other notable restrictions include prohibition of even talking about the work to be done on the morrow (CD 10:19) and if a man falls into water, he cannot be rescued using equipment such as rope and ladder (CD 11:16-17).[16] The penalty for violating the Sabbath by doing any work on it was death (Jub. 2:25, 27, 50:8, 13).[17]

Sabbath in the Period of the NT and the Rabbinic Judaism

Jesus, time and again, enters into conflict with the religious leaders of His time regarding the Sabbath observance because they had made the day absolutely burdensome. The Pharisaic tradition is the predecessor of Rabbinic Judaism and in the period of the Rabbinic Judaism, the Sabbath regulations took extreme measures. The Rabbis provided detailed instructions particularly regarding the prohibition of work that the day became almost unbearable with the restrictions. For instance, Mishnah *Shabbat* 7:2 lists thirty-nine general categories of work that are prohibited on the Sabbath, viz., sowing, ploughing, reaping, binding sheaves, threshing, winnowing, selecting (fit from unfit produce or crops), grinding, sifting, kneading, baking, shearing wool, washing it, beating it, dyeing it, spinning, weaving, making two loops, weaving two threads, separating two threads, tying (a knot), untying (a knot), sewing two stitches, tearing in order to sew two stitches, trapping a deer, slaughtering it, flaying it, salting it, curing its hide, scraping it, cutting it up, writing two letters, erasing two letters in order to write two letters, building, tearing down, putting out a fire, kindling a fire, hitting with a hammer, and transporting an object from one domain to another.[18] The Rabbis turned the Sabbath into what the Torah and the OT as a whole had never envisioned. The words of Jesus ring in the ears when one hears the Sabbath regulations of the Mishnah: "The Sabbath was made for man, not man for the Sabbath" (Mark 2:27). Let alone Rabbinic Judaism, the NT too is unambiguous about the primacy of cessation from work on the Sabbath although the regulations are not spelled out clearly as is done in the Mishnah. Among other acts, Jesus' healings are seen as work (e.g., John 5:1-18, 9:16) and disciples' plucking the heads of grain is seen as work (Mark 2:23-24), and hence are considered violations of the

Sabbath. After Jesus' burial, the women waited for the first day to visit the tomb with spices; but "on the sabbath they rested according to the commandment" (Luke 23:56 NRSV).

However, synagogues are found everywhere in the NT and the Jewish people were expected to attend one on the Sabbath. Jesus, His disciples, Apostle Paul all attended synagogue on the Sabbath. Synagogue attendance on the Sabbath is a given in the NT; and this is true of the period of Rabbinic Judaism as well. The Sabbath service included prayer and study of the Scripture—reading of a text often followed by a homily (see Lewis 161; Scott 140, 142; Flusser 22; cf. Luke 4:16f).[19]

From our discussion thus far, it is clear that the Sabbath in the OT was meant to be a day of rest—cessation from work—without any religious requirements for the general populace. Harrelson is clear: "It is the absence of religious duties to be performed on the Sabbath that makes the day so striking. . . . But nowhere do we find specifications of what ought positively to be done on the Sabbath. Traditions will develop that explain the way in which the Sabbath is to be observed; . . ." (84). Among the traditions developed at a much later period is corporate worship with the development of the synagogues.

Sabbath and the Early Church

Although Christianity seems to be distinct from Judaism, there is no denying that the latter has heavily influenced the former in multiple ways.[20] As Lewis states, "The church arose from the bosom of first century Judaism. Its earliest members were Jews" (157). The apostles and the early church—which comprised of Jews—continued to observe the Sabbath by attending the synagogue (Acts 13:14, 17:1-2, 18:4, 9:2, 22:19, 26:11) together with the "Christian fellowship" on Sundays (Acts 20:7; cf. John 20:19, 26; 1 Cor. 16:2). Earlier, Jesus, a faithful Jew, too observed Sabbath and attended synagogues (Mt. 12:9-14; Mark 1:21-28; Luke 4:16f). However, the spread of the church among the gentiles raised questions concerning the observance of the Torah, more precisely of the issues such as circumcision and food laws (cf. Acts 15). Slowly, Christianity became more of a gentile religion than Jewish which caused it to part ways from Judaism (so also Cohen 161). Several other factors contributed to the parting of ways between Judaism-Synagogue and Christianity-Church. For instance, Davies shows that the close relationship of the early days between the two gradually broke down and became even antagonistic as time passed by due to factors such as Hellenization and imperialization of the Church (235-39). Nonetheless, it is true that "[d]espite what history and theology have made of their relationship, Christianity was born within Judaism and is an expression of it. Fed on the milk of Judaism, it is bone of its bone" (Davies 236). In fact, Boccaccini considers Rabbinic Judaism and Christianity equally "Judaisms"—diverse developments of ancient Judaism (15-18). For Murphy, the two are "siblings" whose common parent is Second Temple Judaism (9).

However, what concerns us the most here is the manner in which the Sabbath observance of the Jews, particularly in relation to the synagogue, has influenced Christian observance of the "Lord's day." The Church undoubtedly borrowed from the Synagogue the elements of a worship service, viz., prayer, reading of Scripture, and sermon.[21] The church began emphasizing corporate worship over the need for rest or cessation of work. The early church met on the first day of the week either early in the morning or late in the evening because the rest of the day had to be spent on work; only in 321 CE with the verdict of Constantine to make Sunday a holiday in his empire could the first day also become the day of rest for Christians (see Rordorf 154-73; Douma 111). Prior to Constantine's declaration, the Christians were not in a position to observe Sunday as the day of rest. However, Christianity today in general emphasizes corporate worship (or church attendance) and hardly talks about rest even though the day is a public holiday. Church leaders emphasize church attendance usually by appealing to the Sabbath and say nothing about the remainder of the day. The end result is that the only requirement for the lay people when the Sabbath law was originally given, i.e., rest from labor, has been lost. The day of rest ("Sabbath") of the early Israelite religion, as it traversed over millennia through Judaism of the exilic and postexilic periods, has become a day (or an hour or two?) of corporate worship in Christianity; and crucial in the journey is the institution of the synagogues.[22]

Summary

Our study in this chapter has shown that the attempts to find the origin of the Sabbath outside of the Israelites has not been convincing even though several theories have been put forward. The Sabbath is most likely an institution that originated with the people of Israel. In addition, our survey of the Sabbath practice from the time of Moses to the period of Rabbinic Judaism reveals that the Sabbath most probably involved cessation of work alone in the pre-exilic period. However, the communal worship aspect began with the origin of the synagogues in the exilic or postexilic period. No cultic activity was required of the general populace on the Sabbath; only the priests were involved in offering sacrifices at the temple and no communal assembly is required by the OT. With the origin of the synagogues began the element of corporate worship for the ordinary Jews. Early Christians who were Jews (including the apostles) continued to observe the Sabbath by attending the synagogues. However, the church also began gathering in homes on the first day, this being the day of the resurrection of Lord Jesus. The early Christians continued their regular work on the first day with a part of the day devoted to fellowship. The verdict of Constantine in 321 CE allowed rest in addition to corporate worship. Christianity today wrongly emphasizes corporate worship or church attendance based on the Sabbath without the mention of rest from labor.

Endnotes

[1] There have been dissenting voices. For instance, Milgrom (*Leviticus 1-16*, 3-13) believes P to be pre-exilic and Wenham ("Priority of P" 240-58) thinks P predates J. However, P as the latest (late exilic or postexilic) source is still the majority view among source critics. See also n. 2 below.

[2] For helpful discussions, see Baker 804; Wenham, "Pondering" 116-44; Whybray, *Pentateuch* 12-28; Petersen, "Formation of the Pentateuch" 31-45; Van Seters, *Pentateuch* 58-86.

[3] See Bacchiocchi, "Remembering" 71-72; Dressler 22; Robinson, *Origin* 16-19, 150-54; Hasel 850; De Vaux 476-78.

[4] Throughout this work, when the English and Hebrew versification differ, the former is given first followed by the latter enclosed in brackets.

[5] Jastrow, however, holds that these days were not merely taboo days but "favorable-unfavorable" days, i.e., "an intermediate position between a 'favorable' and an 'unfavorable' day" (319-21).

[6] Meek (201-12) and I. Lewy (21-25) believe in a lunar origin of the Sabbath; cf. Jastrow (312-52) who believes that the Sabbath is of Babylonian origin and was originally akin to Babylonian "favorable-unfavorable" days (esp. a day of propitiation of deity), which was later transformed into a day of different character than the Babylonians had ascribed because of Israelites' hostility toward Babylonians and in the attempt to make the day unlike Babylonians'; the Hebrew Sabbath, thus, was transformed because of the Israelite protest of the Babylonian characteristics of the "favorable-unfavorable" days.

[7] See Bacchiocchi, "Remembering" 71; Dressler 22; Robinson, *Origin* 15-16; McCann 248; De Vaux 478-79.

[8] The validity of this understanding of סכות and כיון have been questioned. For instance, see Gevirtz 267-76, and Hallo 15.

[9] Budde (1-15) and Rowley (81-118) believe in Kenite origin of not only the Sabbath but the Yahwistic religion as a whole. See also Gordon 12-16 for supposed relationship between the Sabbath and the Saturn.

[10] See McCann 248; Dressler 23; Hasel 851.

[11] Weber believes in socioeconomic theory (150-51).

[12] See McCann 248; Dressler 23; Robinson, *Origin* 13-15.

[13] H. and J. Lewy (1-146) and Unger (55) believe in the calendric origin.

[14] As noted earlier in the introduction, McKay does not find worship even in the synagogues but this is because her definition of "worship" is highly limited; for her, only a restricted nature of the study of the Scripture qualifies as worship (see "From Evidence" 192, 198-99; *Sabbath and Synagogue* 3-4).

[15] This certainly seems to be the case in the time of Rabbinic Judaism as Edersheim has noted concerning the Sabbath day: "Hence, not only were fasting and mourning strictly prohibited [by the Rabbis], but food, dress, and every manner of enjoyment, not incompatible with abstinence from work, were prescribed to render the day pleasurable" (136).

[16] For more on Sabbath regulations, see CD 10:14-11:18.

[17] See Jub. 2:29-30 and 50:6-13 for lists of works forbidden on the Sabbath.

[18] See Neusner 187-88; see 179-208 for a complete English translation of the Mishnah *Shabbat*.

[19] McKay does not find worship in the synagogues even in the NT (see *Sabbath and Synagogue* 132-75); again, this is because of her extremely narrow definition of worship.

[20] For example, see Lewis 154-63; R. Hicks 107-17.

[21] See Filson 86, 88; Millgram 437; Lewis 161; Blomberg, "Sabbath as Fulfilled," *Perspectives* 307. However, the influence goes beyond the elements of a worship service, see Filson 85-88 and R. Hicks 112-16 for brief coverage of the influence of both the temple and the synagogues on the churches. Burtchaell believes that the synagogue had influence on the church even in the latter's "community organization" (see 180ff). For instance, one of the sentences in Burtchaell's conclusion reads, "It is fair

to say that the Jews who formed the archetypal churches followed the basic structural lineaments of community organization already familiar to them in the synagogue" (340). Davies portrays the relationship between synagogue and church as mother and daughter (237).

[22] It must be noted here that Sunday or any particular day is not the issue. Majority of the world has weekly pubic holiday on Sunday, so the churches meet for worship on that day. However, there are nations where the weekly holiday is not on Sunday (e.g., Muslim nations) and the churches meet there on the respective weekly holiday. The issue is that Christians, irrespective of the day, have made the weekly holiday into an hour or two of worship by appealing to the Sabbath regulation but have lost the real meaning of the Sabbath.

Chapter 2

Weekly Sabbath

This chapter's aim is to exegetically study the key passages/verses in the OT that deal with the commandments related to weekly Sabbath and its observances by the people of Israel. As mentioned earlier, the study will be selective, focusing on those texts that contribute most to our understanding of the day's requirements and practices. Many OT texts on the Sabbath are simply indictments for not observing the Sabbath or for profaning it, or positively, commandments to observe it or consecrate it, without any further elucidation. As such, these texts will not be studied because they do not contribute to our understanding of the day's requirements and/or practices. The original audience of these messages, it appears, understood what was meant without need for further explanation. Fuller passages will first be studied beginning with the earliest appearance in the Bible; this will be followed by individual verses. Moreover, a simple schema will be followed: first, the texts dealing with the Sabbath commandments; second, those that deal with its enforcements or observances; third, those that are believed to mention worship on the Sabbath;

and finally the texts that do mention worship. Of course, in some texts command and observance intermingle.

Exodus 16:5, 22-30

Exodus 16 as a whole has to do with the provision of food in the wilderness. The Israelites grumble concerning the lack of food and YHWH provides them with manna and quails, and interspersed in the account is the idea of the Sabbath. Durham rightly says that Exod. 16 deals with provision in that Yahweh provides physical nourishment for His people in the manna and the quails, and spiritual nourishment in the Sabbath rest (216, 223). Hence, it would be ideal to deal with the entire chapter but that is beyond the scope of our study save to present a brief overview of the text.

Text and Context

Source critics see at least two sources (J and P) combined in Exod. 16 (e.g., Baden 491-504; Hyatt 173-74; Noth, *Exodus* 131-32). According to Baden, the J version is pre-Sinaitic and the P post-Sinaitic. The two have been combined and the latter moved forward from somewhere between Num. 14:35 and 20:1 (Baden 499-500). Similarly, some see combined in the story two traditions (e.g., Geller 5-16) and some three (e.g., Robinson, *Origin* 223-26). Whatever the sources and the traditions that the author-redactor might have drawn upon, the narrative as it stands now develops along a clear plot normal to OT narratives: background (v. 1), crisis (vv. 2-12), resolution (vv. 13-30), and conclusion with a gloss (vv. 31-36). As mentioned earlier, our focus will be on the final form of the text and we will concentrate on vv. 5, 22-30 because these verses deal with the issue of Sabbath. The narrative is placed prior to the Sinai event.

This passage is the first recorded incident of the Israelites' observance of the Sabbath in the Bible. Having been delivered from Egyptian bondage and on their way to Sinai, the children of Israel complain about the lack of food after leaving their oasis at Elim following the water crisis (15:22-27). YHWH responds to their complaint and promises to provide food everyday but commands the people to refrain from collecting it on the seventh day because it is the Sabbath. In fact, the manna that was available every morning in the form of the dew around the camp, YHWH says, will not be available on the Sabbath (vv. 25, 26, 27). They were to collect a double portion of their daily quota on the sixth day so that it would be sufficient for the Sabbath day as well (vv. 5, 22). To enable the Israelites to keep the Sabbath, YHWH performed a miracle, presumably a weekly miracle. (The availability of manna every day is in itself a great miracle as well). While the manna that some people kept overnight on a day other than the seventh rotted (v. 20), what was kept from the sixth day until the seventh did not (v. 24). YHWH must be serious about the Sabbath!

Command

The command for the seventh day is to not leave their tents (v. 29b);[1] in other words, the Israelites were to rest (v. 30). No other requirement is prescribed for the day in the text. No cult, no assembly, nothing! Hyatt states, "This is the earliest mention of the Sabbath, and also the earliest observance of the Sabbath by the Israelites (. . .). It is significant that here the Sabbath is considered to be a day of cessation from labour; that seems to be the oldest conception of the Sabbath, which eventually became a day of religious observance" (178). Yes, the tabernacle had not yet been set up and this *could* be the reason for the absence of the cult. An assembly, however, would be possible (cf. vv. 9-12). Hyatt thinks that the incident could have actually happened after the giving of the law at Sinai particularly in light of vv. 10, 32-34, which seem to presuppose the existence of the tabernacle and the ark of the covenant (174, 175). The phrase קָרְבוּ לִפְנֵי יְהֹוָה (v. 9) is a technical term referring to the assembling at the tabernacle, the appearance of כְּבוֹד יְהוָה (v. 10) is used either in the context of Sinai or of the tabernacle, the phrase לִפְנֵי יְהוָה (v. 33) refers to being before the tabernacle, the tabernacle being the place of YHWH's residence, and the הָעֵדֻת (v. 34) is clearly a reference to the ark of the covenant which held the tablets (Baden 496-98).[2] Hence, it is possible that there is a chronological displacement here and that is not uncommon in the OT. Durham, however, commenting on the reference to the ark in vv. 32-34, says that the reason for this is "an important theological purpose which overrides considerations of logical and chronological sequence" (226). Obvious is the fact that the account was written in the form we have in the period after the Conquest (cf. v. 35) and when the omer for the measurement prevalent at the time of the event was out of use, and this necessitated the gloss in v. 36. Hence, it is more probable that the event predated the Sinai episode but the author-redactor who gave the chapter its present form much later wrote it in light of the Sinai episode. Of more interest to us is the fact that the Israelites are commanded to refrain from gathering manna and possibly cooking as well on the Sabbath (more below) without any command to "worship."

Miracle(s)?

Many believe that vv. 17-18 suggest a miracle in that no matter how much each gathered, it turned out to be what they actually could have eaten on the day (e.g., Noth, *Exodus* 135) or each one happened to gather an omer (e.g., Durham 220, 223). However, it is more probable that each one gathered as much as they needed measuring it with an omer (cf. vv. 4, 21; see Stuart, *Exodus* 379). That such is probably the case is also hinted by the "test" in v. 4b. If what was gathered automatically turned out to be the prescribed quantity, then the testing makes no sense. The testing in the context (see v. 4a) has to be whether or not the people will trust God enough to gather only what was needed for the day without hoarding it for the future.[3]

Similarly, Childs thinks that the people gathered as much on the sixth day as they did on other days unaware that they were to gather double portion, but it became doubled to their surprise (cf. v. 5) and this is the reason the leaders came to Moses (v. 22) for clarification (*Exodus* 290; cf. Durham 219-20). The inference is that there was a miracle in that what the people gathered, YHWH doubled (contra Houtman 2: 347, 332; Ferris 194). However, a more likely situation is that the people gathered twice the measure on the sixth day because Moses had told them to do so; they followed Moses' command but were not told the reason for the same, which brought the leaders to Moses who, then, provides the rationale behind the command (vv. 22f) (so also Sarna 90, 87). In other words, Moses creates suspense and anticipation on the part of the Israelites who must be wondering what the reason could be for such a command, especially in light of the fact that whatever had been kept overnight earlier was spoiled (v. 20; cf. Houtman 2: 347).

What is the guarantee that such would not happen again? The leaders naturally desire explanation; so do all the people that they represent. Moses does all this to teach them an important lesson—the lesson of the Sabbath. In other words, it was Moses' pedagogical tactic (so also Ben Meir, *Exodus* 176-77). Or should we say that the author-redactor is a literary artist; the elucidation for the suspense he had introduced in v. 5 has to wait until vv. 23f? The readers are in for a literary treat. A major literary feature of this chapter is suspense and this is used in order to highlight the importance of the Sabbath. Moreover, the "test" mentioned in v. 4b probably has a further aspect in light of v. 5 (and vv. 22-26), namely, to see whether the Israelites will obey the command to not attempt gathering on the Sabbath.

The view that the people gathered the same quantity on the sixth day as they did on the other five days, which YHWH doubled, is inspired by v. 5; v. 22 is very clear that the *people* gathered twice the amount (לָקְטוּ לֶחֶם מִשְׁנֶה) on the sixth day. Let us look at v. 5 closely:

וְהָיָה בַּיּוֹם הַשִּׁשִּׁי וְהֵכִינוּ אֵת אֲשֶׁר־יָבִיאוּ וְהָיָה מִשְׁנֶה עַל אֲשֶׁר־יִלְקְטוּ יוֹם יוֹם

But it shall be on the sixth day that they shall prepare what they bring in, and it is to be double of what they gather day by day[4] (cf. NIV; Houtman 2: 330).

Most translate the verse along this line: 'On the sixth day, *when* they prepare what they bring in, *it will be* twice as much as they gather on other days' (see NRSV, NASB, ESV). This translation is arrived at by taking וְהֵכִינוּ . . . וְהָיָה as a conditional clause. However, it is more probable as Houtman (2: 331) proposes that these two verbs introduce clauses that are coordinate to the clause introduced by the first וְהָיָה. Moreover, v. 22 indicates that our translation is more appropriate.

Message

Whatever one believes concerning the miracle(s), what is of greater concern to us is that an important lesson is given to the Israelites here, i.e., to refrain from work on the Sabbath and trust YHWH for provision. The practice would then be carried on into the Promised Land. Exod. 16 anticipates the giving of the Sabbath law at Sinai and its observance in the God-given land perpetually. An important point to be noted here is that not only the people are commanded to refrain from work on the Sabbath but YHWH too refrains from work, i.e., from providing the food, as Brueggemann puts it quite interestingly: "Not only must the people refrain from working on the sabbath, but also God's own bakeries are closed for the day" ("Exodus" 814; see also Enns 325; Houtman 2: 349). Even if the Israelites refuse to keep the command and seek to collect manna on the Sabbath, as some apparently did (v. 27), they would find none because YHWH would provide none. We see here an allusion to Genesis 2:1-3; people's Sabbath observance entails *imitatio Dei*.[5]

Concerning the cessation of work on the Sabbath, a question which is frequently raised in light of v. 23 that we cannot overlook is whether all the manna gathered on the sixth day was to be prepared the same day? If so, the Sabbath involved refraining from gathering as well as cooking. Or was cooking allowed on the Sabbath such that the portion to be eaten on the day was kept "unprepared" from the previous day? (Later Jewish tradition forbids cooking on the Sabbath and whatever has to be eaten on the day is to be prepared on the sixth day but this does not necessarily reflect the situation in Exod. 16.). Beuken argues at length that the portion for the Sabbath day was kept uncooked (7ff; cf. Sarna 90; Noth, *Exodus* 136). Others believe that the portion for both the days was cooked on Friday (Houtman 2: 348-49; W. Kaiser, "Exodus" 402, 403). Enns, in the same vein, believes that the baking is for manna and boiling for quail, and this is "commanded" to prevent the food from being spoiled until the next day (326 including n. 12). I, however, believe that the food not getting spoiled on the Sabbath is a miracle, irrespective of whether it was kept raw or cooked; it is not clear from v. 20 that those who earlier kept some remaining until the next day kept raw food. Moreover, Enns' assigning baking to manna and boiling to quail seems unwarranted because the manna could be prepared in multiple ways (see Num. 11:8; Houtman 2: 348) and also the manna alone seems to be the subject of discussion here, not the meat. Nonetheless, I do believe that all the food that was gathered on the sixth day was cooked on the same day, particularly in light of v. 5: "But it shall be on the sixth day that they shall prepare what they bring in. . ." (see my translation above). The verse appears to suggest that whatever they bring in, they shall prepare on the sixth day (cf. my discussion of coordinate clauses above). In any case, the overall lesson of refraining from daily work and trusting YHWH for the provision is achieved. The significant point to be noted here, as we have already mentioned, is that the story records no instruction for "worship" on the Sabbath. Despite this, some take for granted that worship was a requirement of the Sabbath. For instance, Stuart states that the Sabbath "is not just a day of resting from work but a day of refocused service toward the holy, that is, toward God. . . . The time and energy normally spent gathering manna could now be spent on

God's worship and, to some extent, not spent at all" (*Exodus* 381). Stuart, I believe, reads his view into the text; he requires time and energy to be spent in God's service/worship. The text, however, does not mention such. The day is to be spent ceasing from daily work; in this case, from gathering manna. Stuart is more faithful to the text when he writes that the time and energy is "to some extent, not [be] spent at all."

Exodus 31:12-17, 35:2-3

Exod. 31:12-17 is crucial to our study since it introduces a special aspect of the Sabbath, i.e., the Sabbath is a sign (אוֹת) of the perpetual covenant between YHWH and His chosen people Israel (cf. Ezek. 20:12). Source critics attribute the pericope to P. However, there are versions of this. For instance, Knohl sees the text as coming entirely from the Holiness School; in other words, the passage is an H text which, to Knohl, is a late hand in P material (see esp. 65-66, 73-74). On the other hand, Olyan sees it as a likely composite of H (vv. 12-15) and P (vv. 16-17), but contra Knohl and in line with OT scholars in general, he believes H to be earlier than P (201-09). Whatever the sources and/or redactions, the present form of the text has a clear structure and its placement in the book is intentional.

Context and Structure

The Sabbath commandment forms an inclusio for the story of the great apostasy of the Israelites, namely, the Golden Calf incident (Exod. 32-34). Literarily, this probably means that even though there was a setback, the covenant is unbroken (cf. P. Williamson 101 n. 14; Enns 545). More importantly, the last instruction Moses receives from YHWH on Mount Sinai concerns the Sabbath (31:12-17) and the first instruction Moses gives to the Israelites after descending from Sinai is the

Sabbath (35:1-3). In addition, the instructions for constructing the tabernacle (25:1-31:11) is followed by the Sabbath regulations and the actual act of constructing the tabernacle (35:4-40:33) is preceded by the instruction on the Sabbath. All these mean that the Sabbath is important to the author-redactor of the book of Exodus. He has arranged his writing in such a way that the Sabbath receives prominence. The juxtaposition of Sabbath regulations with the command for tabernacle construction likely shows that the Sabbath takes precedence over the construction of the sanctuary (Ben Meir, *Exodus* 392; R. A. Cole 234). Knohl, however, adds that it is "to magnify the Sabbath and to place its sanctity on the same level as that of the Sanctuary" (74). Both interpretations are valid; they are complementary and are appropriate in the context. If so, then this passage is very crucial for our understanding of the Sabbath. The person who considers the Sabbath to take precedence over the work for the tabernacle construction and regards the sanctity of the Sabbath on par with that of the sanctuary will be very cautious to carefully spell out the instructions for the same. Hence, we now turn to a closer look at the text in question.[6]

Exod. 31:12-17 is arranged in a chiastic structure (cf. Brueggemann, "Exodus" 923):

Prologue: YHWH commands Moses (vv. 12-13a)

A Sabbath observance as a sign (v. 13b)

  B Death penalty for Sabbath violators (v. 14)

    C Sabbath regulation: six days work and seventh day rest (v. 15a)

  B' Death penalty for Sabbath violators (v. 15b)

A' Sabbath observance as a sign (vv. 16-17a)

Epilogue: YHWH worked six days and rested on the seventh (v. 17b)

The structure above shows that the focal point of the passage is rest from work on the seventh day (C). The validity of this conclusion is also attested by 35:1-3 where Moses carries out YHWH's command of announcing to the Israelites what has been spoken to him in this passage; 31:15 alone is repeated in 35:2 (more below). Sabbath observance is a sign of the covenant between YHWH and the people of Israel (A/A') and thus the observance is so crucial that its violation should be penalized by death (B/B'). If so, how is the Sabbath to be observed? By resting or refraining from work (C). No cult or worship is prescribed. Miller sees two activities in v. 14, namely, profaning the Sabbath and working on the Sabbath (*Ten Commandments* 152). Likewise, some see a discrepancy in the penalty prescribed: excommunication from the community (14c) and execution (14b, 15b). However, there is only one activity and one penalty in the text as shown below:

מוֹת יוּמָת	מְחַלְלֶיהָ
וְנִכְרְתָה הַנֶּפֶשׁ הַהִוא מִקֶּרֶב עַמֶּיהָ	כִּי כָּל־הָעֹשֶׂה בָהּ מְלָאכָה
מוֹת יוּמָת	כָּל־הָעֹשֶׂה מְלָאכָה בְּיוֹם הַשַּׁבָּת

The three phrases are parallel; and hence the text is clear that the Sabbath is profaned by working on it and the penalty of this is cutting off the perpetrator from the community by execution—one act of violation and one penalty. P. Williamson is correct that there is no discrepancy; the penalty is "exclusion from the covenant community through death, not merely physical expulsion" (102 n. 16).

Omission and Addition

Omissions, additions, and subtle changes in repeated material are crucial. Moses carries out YHWH's command of 31:12-17 in 35:1-3. What is interesting here is that Moses (or author-redactor) is very brief when he conveys the Sabbath command to the Israelites. He omits some detail and as mentioned above, highlights only one thing, namely, six days of work and rest on the seventh, followed by the provision of death penalty if work is done on the Sabbath (v. 2). The sign element which seems crucial to 31:12-17 is not mentioned in chapter 35. Verse 2 of the latter is almost a verbatim repetition of 31:15. The likely reason for the omission of other details and mention of 31:15 alone is that the author believes this to be the crux of the Sabbath, namely, rest on the seventh day. The regulation is so serious that working on the day is to be penalized by death. The seriousness of the command is also highlighted by מוֹת יוּמָת, an emphatic construction: infinitive absolute followed by imperfect (14a, 15b). The phrase is better translated, "... shall surely be put to death" (on the emphatic use of the infinitive absolute, see *IBHS* 584-88 §35.3.1; *WHS* 85 §205).

The author, however, adds the prohibition of kindling fire (v. 3), which is absent in 31:12-17. The reason is not given. The prohibition follows the words כָּל־הָעֹשֶׂה בוֹ מְלָאכָה יוּמָת ("anyone who does work on it shall be put to death") in 35:2, which suggests that it is an explanation to clarify in some way the prohibition of work. Some believe the restriction concerned the blacksmiths' kindling of fire for the construction of the tabernacle (e.g., Hyatt 329). However, as Houtman (3: 588) also contends, the phrase בְּכֹל מֹשְׁבֹתֵיכֶם ("in all your dwellings") invalidates this interpretation. The phrase suggests that the words are applicable to all of the Israelite settlements.

Therefore, the prohibition of kindling fire here most probably is at the household level, especially cooking food (so also Stuart, *Exodus* 749; Durham 475; cf. Phillips, "Woodgatherer" 127; Levine, *Numbers 1-20*, 399; Ashley 291; Dozeman 128). In fact, Houtman notes: "Excluded from the prohibition is the sanctuary" (3: 591). Houtman's interpretation makes perfect sense in light of the command for sacrifices on the Sabbath at the sanctuary (cf. Stuart, *Exodus* 749). The construction of the tabernacle is surely to be halted on the Sabbath. The juxtaposition of the Sabbath command with the tabernacle shows that the Sabbath observance by abstaining from work takes precedence over tabernacle construction (cf. Jenson 195). However, once the construction is over and the cult is in place, kindling fire on the Sabbath at the sanctuary is not only permitted but commanded (Num. 28:9-10).

Why, then, is kindling fire for household use singled out? Stuart, I believe, is correct that cooking daily food is so basic that people might be tempted to undertake it. In addition, it would also be easy to justify cooking by citing that eating was not prohibited on the Sabbath, rather YHWH had sanctioned it by providing food for the Sabbath on the sixth day itself (Exod. 16) (Stuart, *Exodus* 749). Thus, the prohibition of kindling fire is simply a clarification of prohibition of work on the Sabbath. All of this means that 35:1-3 considers rest on the seventh day as central to the Sabbath observance because the author singles out this aspect while reiterating 31:12-17 and even adds a clarifying statement to make his point.[7]

In the final analysis, the passages show that the only requirement of the Sabbath is cessation from work. Failure to do so should result in extermination. There is no mention whatsoever of any cultic/worship requirement—sacrifices or assemblies. Rest alone is a must.

God Rested and Was Refreshed

The last phrase of v. 17 reads: וּבַיּוֹם הַשְּׁבִיעִי שָׁבַת וַיִּנָּפַשׁ ("and on the seventh day, [God] ceased/rested and was refreshed"). The last word (וַיִּנָּפַשׁ) in particular has raised enormous interest. The verb נפשׁ appears only thrice in the OT and all of them in the Niphal (Exod. 23:12, 31:17; 2 Sam. 16:14). Brueggemann says that the verb can be translated in the passive ("refreshed," etc.) or in the reflexive ("refreshed self," etc.); the meaning, however, is still the same ("Exodus" 924). The verb has the idea of catching one's breath (see Fredericks 133). Why did God rest (cf. Gen. 2:2-3)? Does God need rest and refreshing? Was He tired after creating such a magnificent and complex universe? Brueggemann has no doubt that such was the case: "The *inescapable* inference is that in six days of creation God worked very hard, and God's own self had been diminished through that exertion. . . . For a moment here, the text lets the reader see God from the other side, the side of frailty and vulnerability" ("Exodus" 924, emphasis mine; cf. ibid. 845). These are strong words but I believe Brueggemann is overdrawing from the text. The Bible mentions, for instance, YHWH neither sleeps nor slumbers (Ps. 121:3-4), which means He does not need rest. As Moltmann says, "God does not 'rest' in the sense of taking a break now and then, in order to gather strength for further tasks" (4). What, then, are we to make of the concepts of YHWH resting and being refreshed? The most logical answer is that He was *modeling* in order to communicate to human beings that they need periodic rest (cf. Olson 52, 65; House 8; Miller, *Ten Commandments* 126). In other words, they are anthropomorphisms used to motivate people to take time to rest and be refreshed. God is used as an example, a model, for humans to imitate. Dressler rightly says that the "anthropomorphic terms are employed not to tell us about God's activities but to inform us what man is to do." He adds: "God needs no rest or refreshing as His strength never fails" (Dressler 28, 39 n. 62). Exod. 23:12 uses the same verb (וַיִּנָּפֵשׁ) to communicate literally that humans (as well as cattle) need periodic rest and refreshing, and spelled out are the most vulnerable of the society. "If God needed rest (and refreshing), how much more we mortal human beings?" is not a correct interpretation of the biblical text.

Message

The following are the main points of the passage:

1. Sabbath observance is a sign of the perpetual covenant between YHWH and Israel (vv. 13, 16-17).

2. Sabbath is holy (vv. 14, 15).

3. Working on the Sabbath profanes the day and this necessitates execution (vv. 14, 15; cf. 35:2).

4. Keeping the Sabbath means ceasing from work, i.e., resting; and this is an act of imitating God (vv. 14-15, 17; cf. Gen. 2:1-3).

Here again, there is no mention whatsoever of any cultic activity, either in the form of sacrifices or some sort of communal gathering/worship. The matter is doubly important because the Sabbath regulations are given here in the context of the sanctuary construction—the seat of Israelite cultic activities. If any place was most suitable for the author to prescribe cultic regulations for the Sabbath, this is the one. Yet, the only requirement is rest or cessation from work following YHWH's example; whoever breaks the Sabbath by doing any work on it is liable of the death penalty. Commenting on this passage, Brueggemann concurs: "It has no interest in things liturgical or priestly, nor is it preoccupied with presence. It is, rather, concerned with *sabbath as rest (and not worship)*, a concern that touches primarily the public, economic sphere of Israel's life" ("Exodus" 923, emphasis mine). Some disagree. Enns commenting on the text writes, "Weekly Sabbath worship is on holy ground [tabernacle] in holy time [Sabbath]" (546). Stuart, in the same vein, comments that the mention of the Sabbath in the current context means "the Tabernacle was for worship; worship occurred weekly, on the Sabbath; and if the Sabbath were not properly observed, worship would not properly take place; . . ." (*Exodus* 653). There are problems in Enns' and Stuart's interpretations. First, the worship took place at the tabernacle daily, not merely weekly on the Sabbath. The only difference is that there were additional sacrifices on the Sabbath. Second, the weekly sacrifices/worship was to be performed by the priests and, contrary to what Enns and Stuart imply, no "worship" is prescribed for the general populace.[8] Moreover, the juxtaposition of the Sabbath command with the command for tabernacle construction does not mean what Stuart makes of it; rather the implication is, as discussed above, 'the sacred time takes precedence over the sacred space.' This also means that the tabernacle construction needs to be halted on the Sabbath. Rest or cessation of work is the requirement of the Sabbath.

Sabbath and Decalogue

The centrality of the Sabbath commandment in the Decalogue has been widely accepted (e.g., Miller, *Ten Commandments* 127-

29). The interpretation of this command, however, is the most debated among the ten. The two versions of the Decalogue (Exod. 20 and Deut. 5) provide us with the rationale for Sabbath observance. Moreover, they also provide us a clear explanation of the purpose of the Sabbath. Let us first look at the rationale. The two versions, as R. Sherman holds, are theologically complementary although a historian might see two different sources/traditions behind them (40). Kahn agrees that the Deuteronomic version is not a "correction or parallel to Exodus, but . . . an enriching explanation, an expansion and a development" (243; cf. Miller, *Ten Commandments* 118).

Rationale for the Sabbath

Imitatio Dei is the first basis for keeping the Sabbath. The book of Exodus looks back to the creation in Genesis in providing the rationale for the Sabbath (Exod. 20:11). The Israelites are to keep the Sabbath because YHWH rested on the seventh day after completing the creation in six days (Gen. 2:1-3). They are to imitate Him. In keeping the Sabbath, God's people acknowledge Him as the Creator and follow His example in rejoicing in the beautiful creation He has brought into existence (see Hamilton 903; Moltmann 4). In short, the first rationale is: God rested; imitate Him.

The book of Deuteronomy looks back to the exodus as the rationale for the Sabbath (Deut. 5:15). The Israelites are to keep the Sabbath because they were slaves in Egypt and are now delivered. The Sabbath, then, provided rest for everyone, not the least for the slaves and even the cattle. Slaves do not have a day off. They need to work seven days a week. With the Sabbath law, God was telling the Israelites to treat the slaves fairly and give them rest. They are not to follow their experience in Egypt of not having rest when they were slaves. In short, the second rationale is: Egyptians oppressed you; do not imitate them.

When something is added, omitted, or altered from the earlier version in repeated material, it is significant. Moses repeats the Decalogue in Deuteronomy to a new generation forty years after its original giving to the previous generation at Sinai. In repeating the fourth commandment—the Sabbath—he gives different rationale for its observance than was given in the Exodus version. The difference is more substantial because Moses is the man behind both the versions. He receives the commandments from YHWH at Sinai in the Exodus account and he is the one who recites it in the Deuteronomic account. In light of the fact that the Israelites are finally going to live a settled life in the Promised Land, Moses gives an additional basis for keeping the law that would *guarantee* rest not only for the well-to-do such as the slave owners but also for the slaves (poor and vulnerable), especially repeated and reemphasized by the latter part of 5:14 (more below). In keeping the Sabbath, therefore, God's people also acknowledge Him as the Redeemer.

Purpose of the Sabbath

The primary purpose for giving the Sabbath was to provide humans rest from labor. In the two versions of the Decalogue, even though the rationales are different, the purpose is the same—to refrain from work, and rest (Exod. 20:9-10; Deut. 5:13-14). Moreover, even in the Exodus version the basis for keeping the Sabbath is God's *resting* (Exod. 20:11). Comparing the two versions will clarify the issue (see Table 1).

Table 1: Sabbath Commandment in the Decalogue

	Exodus 20	Deuteronomy 5
Command Exod. 20:8 Deut. 5:12	זָכוֹר אֶת־יוֹם הַשַּׁבָּת לְקַדְּשׁוֹ: Remember the Sabbath day to keep it holy.	שָׁמוֹר אֶת־יוֹם הַשַּׁבָּת לְקַדְּשׁוֹ כַּאֲשֶׁר צִוְּךָ יְהוָה אֱלֹהֶיךָ: Observe the Sabbath day to keep it holy as YHWH your God commanded you.
Purpose Exod. 20:9-10 Deut. 5:13-14	שֵׁשֶׁת יָמִים תַּעֲבֹד וְעָשִׂיתָ כָּל־מְלַאכְתֶּךָ: וְיוֹם הַשְּׁבִיעִי שַׁבָּת לַיהוָה אֱלֹהֶיךָ לֹא־תַעֲשֶׂה כָל־מְלָאכָה אַתָּה וּבִנְךָ־וּבִתֶּךָ עַבְדְּךָ וַאֲמָתְךָ וּבְהֶמְתֶּךָ וְגֵרְךָ אֲשֶׁר בִּשְׁעָרֶיךָ: Six days you shall labor and do all your work but the seventh day is a Sabbath to YHWH your God. You shall *not do any work*—you or your son or your daughter; your male slave or your female slave; or your cattle or your sojourner who is within your gates.	שֵׁשֶׁת יָמִים תַּעֲבֹד וְעָשִׂיתָ כָּל־מְלַאכְתֶּךָ: וְיוֹם הַשְּׁבִיעִי שַׁבָּת לַיהוָה אֱלֹהֶיךָ לֹא תַעֲשֶׂה כָל־מְלָאכָה אַתָּה וּבִנְךָ־וּבִתֶּךָ וְעַבְדְּךָ־וַאֲמָתֶךָ **וְשׁוֹרְךָ וַחֲמֹרְךָ** וְכָל־בְּהֶמְתֶּךָ וְגֵרְךָ אֲשֶׁר בִּשְׁעָרֶיךָ **לְמַעַן יָנוּחַ עַבְדְּךָ וַאֲמָתְךָ כָּמוֹךָ:** Six days you shall labor and do all your work but the seventh day is a Sabbath to YHWH your God. You shall *not do any work*—you or your son or your daughter; or your male slave or your female slave; or **your ox or your donkey** or any of your cattle; or your sojourner who is within your gates; **so that your male slave and your female slave may *rest* just like you.**
Rationale Exod. 20:11 Deut. 5:15	כִּי שֵׁשֶׁת־יָמִים עָשָׂה יְהוָה אֶת־הַשָּׁמַיִם וְאֶת־הָאָרֶץ אֶת־הַיָּם וְאֶת־כָּל־אֲשֶׁר־בָּם וַיָּנַח בַּיּוֹם הַשְּׁבִיעִי עַל־כֵּן בֵּרַךְ יְהוָה אֶת־יוֹם הַשַּׁבָּת וַיְקַדְּשֵׁהוּ: For *in* six days YHWH made the heavens and the earth; the sea and all that is in them, and He *rested* on the seventh day. Therefore, YHWH blessed the Sabbath day and consecrated it.	וְזָכַרְתָּ כִּי־עֶבֶד הָיִיתָ בְּאֶרֶץ מִצְרַיִם וַיֹּצִאֲךָ יְהוָה אֱלֹהֶיךָ מִשָּׁם בְּיָד חֲזָקָה וּבִזְרֹעַ נְטוּיָה עַל־כֵּן צִוְּךָ יְהוָה אֱלֹהֶיךָ לַעֲשׂוֹת אֶת־יוֹם הַשַּׁבָּת: And you shall remember that you were a slave in the land of Egypt, and YHWH your God brought you out from there with a strong hand and with an outstretched arm. Therefore, YHWH your God commanded you to observe the Sabbath day.

An almost a verbatim repetition of the purpose of the Sabbath in Deuteronomy from Exodus is clear. The additions in the Deuteronomic account are given in boldface. Deuteronomy does not add any extra material per se but the final phrase reemphasizes the necessity of the slaves to rest just as the slave owners do. The emphasis is in line with the Deuteronomic rationale that they are to observe the Sabbath by remembering that they were slaves in Egypt who are delivered by YHWH. They are not to treat their slaves as did their overlords in Egypt.

The Sabbath law has a major humanitarian dimension with a concern for the welfare of the slaves. The primary emphasis is on allowing rest to the slaves a day per week. Kahn rightly calls it a "sociological scheme protecting slaves and workers" (240, 243). But the slave owners' need to rest is not excluded. Budde's statement (4) that Deut. 5 requires only slaves and cattle to rest but the masters are not obligated to do so is invalid. The last phrase of Deut. 5:14 reads: לְמַעַן יָנוּחַ עַבְדְּךָ וַאֲמָתְךָ כָּמוֹךָ ("so that your male slave and your female slave may rest *just like you*"; emphasis added). Moreover, the list of those restricted from work begins with אַתָּה (Deut. 5:14; Exod. 20:10). That the well-to-do (e.g., slave owners) rest was taken for granted at the time the commandment was given (cf. Tigay 69; Miller, *Ten Commandments* 130). However, today we live in a world where many of the well-to-do also lack rest. They impose lack of rest upon themselves. Workaholics abound. Work is overvalued. Rest is often taken as idleness or wasting of time. The Sabbath law thus speaks to the well-to-do and the employers not only to give rest to their helpers and employees but also to cultivate the habit of resting themselves.

The Sabbath command in the Decalogue has one concern, i.e., rest from labor. Taken at face value, the texts say nothing about worship, only that it should be kept holy (more below). The centrality of rest or cessation from work is also clear from the structure of the Sabbath command in the two Decalogue passages.

Structure

The structure of the fourth commandment of both versions of the Decalogue sheds light on what is central to the Sabbath. They are both written in chiastic structure.

Exod. 20:8-11 (cf. Doukhan 159):

A Sabbath is holy (8)

  B Work six days but the seventh is the Sabbath (9-10a)

    C Do no work on the seventh day (10b)

  B' God worked for six days and rested the seventh (11a)

A' Sabbath is holy (11b)

The structure clearly shows that the core of the Sabbath commandment is abstention from work on the seventh day for everyone. Moreover, in keeping with the sabbatical nature, seven entries are listed as the subject of Sabbath observance, viz., you, son, daughter, male slave, female slave, cattle, and sojourner (v. 10b). In the Deuteronomic version, 'cattle' has been expanded to 'ox, donkey, or any cattle' (v. 14b).

Deut. 5:12-15 (cf. Doukhan 160):

A Observe the Sabbath (12)

  B Labor/slave (תַּעֲבֹד) six days but the seventh is the Sabbath (13-14a)

    C Do no work on the seventh day (14b)

  B' Remember you were a slave (עֶבֶד) in Egypt (15a)

A' Observe the Sabbath (15b)

At first glance, there seems to be no relation between B and B' but there is. B' is, in essence, saying that when you were slaves in Egypt, you had no rest but had to work seven days a week; now that you have been delivered from slavery, work only six days and rest on the seventh (B). Note the Hebrew root עבד in both: you shall labor (תַּעֲבֹד) only six days (B); remember you were a slave (עֶבֶד) in Egypt (B'). Just as is the case with the Exodus version, here too the center is abstention from work on the seventh day.

Message

Finally, our study of the fourth commandment in the two versions of the Decalogue shows that rest is central to the Sabbath; worship is not prescribed. If there is any worship element, it is *indirect* in the rationale. As one observes the Sabbath and asks him/herself the reason for doing so, the answer will be twofold. First, YHWH rested at creation, which recalls that He is the Creator (Exodus version). Second, YHWH delivered from Egyptian slavery, i.e., He is the Redeemer (Deuteronomic version). This aspect, however, is the reverse effect. In other words, Sabbath observance results from remembering that God ceased work on the seventh day of creation (Exod. 20) and that He delivered the Israelites from slavery in Egypt (Deut. 5). That is, the Israelites are commanded to observe the Sabbath not *so that* they can remember God's creative and redemptive acts (contra Miller, *Ten Commandments* 119, 130) but *as a result* of remembering these divine acts. Sabbath observance is commanded so that they can rest and be refreshed. As the Creator and Redeemer, YHWH deserves worship but the Sabbath command lacks such injunction. Many think otherwise. For instance, Miller, while conceding that the Decalogue only mentions the "not-doing" part of the Sabbath and lacks the "doing" part, still holds that it is to be a day of service to the Lord; this makes the day holy. And this, he says, is to be drawn out from "some clues and ideas" from other portions of the Bible on the Sabbath (Miller, *Ten Commandments* 120).

Moreover, he states, "From the beginning, the point of the commandment is to make sure that time for the worship of God is provided in the midst of human activities" (ibid. 121; cf. Packer 66-68; W. Kaiser, "Exodus" 424). However, the text does not say anything in this regard. Brueggemann correctly comments on this commandment: "There is no mention of worship" ("Exodus" 845). Rest is the requirement.

Numbers 15:32-36

The passage records an incident during the Israelites' wilderness wandering in which a person defiles the Sabbath and is put to death by stoning at the hands of the whole Israelite community. Here we see a concrete application of the law prescribed in Exod. 31:12-17, 35:2-3, and the seriousness of Sabbath violation. The passage follows a lawsuit pattern. A person is caught breaking the law (32), he is taken for trial (33), kept in custody until the verdict is given (34), the verdict is given after consultation, here with God (35), and the verdict is enforced (36).

Text and Context

Source critics attribute the text to H. For instance, Novick believes it to be H material, which was either composed or given its canonical form and setting in the exilic period by building upon a tradition from the wilderness. The purpose of this was to provide an answer to the questions related to the validity or place of the law in the exile (Novick 11). However, the biblical writer has set the passage in the period of Israel's wilderness wandering prior to entering the Promised Land.

The narrative follows legal instructions concerning individual sins (vv. 27-31). Verses 27-29 deal with unintentional sins which are forgiven after offering the prescribed sacrifice,

whereas vv. 30-31 deal with intentional sins which cannot be
forgiven, resulting in the cutting off from the community of
the person committing them. The positioning of the pericope
after the discourse on intentional sins (vv. 30-31) seems to
suggest that the incident in vv. 32-36 is an example of such
sin.[9] Milgrom agrees and holds that if the violation was
unintentional, then "sacrificial expiation" as prescribed in vv.
27-29 would suffice (*Numbers* 410). The phrase used to refer
to intentional sins is בְּיָד רָמָה, "with a high hand" (v. 30). רָמָה
is a participle functioning as an attributive adjective modifying
יָד (cf. *WHS* 88 §215a). Elsewhere the expression is used to
denote the Israelites' bold, defiant march out of Egypt at the
Exodus (Exod. 14:8; Num. 33:3). The portrayal of the sin
involved in our text is that of a blatant, defiant violation of
YHWH's command. R. Harrison writes that the expression
(בְּיָד רָמָה) is "as though the transgressor was about to attack
God or rebel against Him wantonly" (*Numbers* 227). Sabbath
violation is akin to "the act of a raised fist in defiance of the
Lord" or "thumbing his nose at God" (Allen 831).

Inquiry and Penalty

Why was it necessary to inquire of YHWH regarding what is to
be done to the wood gatherer? As did the Rabbis, some believe
it was to find out the mode of execution; the death penalty
was obvious (Ben Meir, *Leviticus and Numbers* 223; Bailey 477;
cf. Owens 126; Jensen 70). Weingreen believes it was needed
because this was a new situation and no clear instruction was
given in the law as to what should be done to such person.
Kindling fire meant execution (Exod. 35:3) but what was to
be done to a wood gatherer was not clear. Therefore, Moses
needed to know two things. First, should gathering wood be
seen as an intent at kindling fire, and hence, an attempt at

breaking the law? Second, does the intent to break the law deserve the same penalty as actually breaking it? Weingreen sees here in its early form the concept of "a fence round the Torah" found in Rabbinic thought.[10] Weingreen pushes his proposal a little too far. The issue is not so much "intent." The simple conclusion that the text allows is the inquiry was required to find out whether gathering wood—presumably to kindle fire—was equivalent to actually kindling it, and hence deserved the same penalty (cf. Ashley 291). The outcome suggests that the question was answered in the affirmative. That the Sabbath was violated was clear; the manner of its violation, however, was not. R. Harrison, however, holds: "The sentence [death penalty] was consistent with existing instructions from God (Ex. 31:14-15; 35:2), which Moses and the Israelites had either forgotten or were reluctant to apply" (*Numbers* 228). I believe that it was rather to find out whether the same penalty applied for gathering wood as it did for making fire.

One question that is frequently raised is: 'Why is there such a severe penalty for a seemingly minor violation?' Robinson believes that it is because the person intended to kindle a "strange fire" for worship of strange gods ("Strange Fire" 301-17). As noted in n. 7 above, his view is highly conjectural. Burnside holds that "the cognitive structures that go into reading the biblical Sabbath laws are narrative and visual, rather than semantic and literal" (45, cf. 50, 51, 55, 60). With this approach, he draws parallel between the violation of Sabbath and slavery in Egypt, based on which he makes assertions such as these: "The Sabbath-breaker's behavior thus signifies a desire to return to Egypt." And, "he shows his rejection of the covenant and the 'sign' of the covenant in favour of a return to Egypt and to Pharaoh's economic conditions" (Burnside 59, 61). His methodology granted, Burnside is still reading too much into the text in which an individual is gathering some wood most probably to kindle fire for cooking food (cf. Levine, *Numbers 1-20*, 399). Moreover, the comparison is stretched beyond its reasonable limits.[11]

Novick, on the other hand, holds that the Israelites felt after the spy incident and their subsequent refusal to inherit the Promised Land that the law was no longer applicable to them, not until they inherited the Land. Moreover, the wood gatherer represented the whole community, i.e., the story is about communal sin, not individual (Novick 4-8). The view is problematic for several reasons. First, nowhere is there even a hint in the Torah that the Israelites felt after their refusal to inherit the Promised Land that they no longer were in covenant with YHWH and needed not keep the law. Second, the story is clearly about the breach of a law by an individual; only he is stoned to death. Two further points are important here: (1) if the sin was communal, the whole community should have been punished, and more importantly, (2) how is it that the participants in the violation of the law are the very ones who throw stones at one perpetrator as an act of just punishment? The most probable reason for the death penalty is that collecting wood was seen as equivalent to kindling fire which was punishable by death (Exod. 35:2-3). Hence, Moses' inquiry of God most likely did not concern the type of punishment or the mode of execution; rather it was to know whether gathering wood was equivalent to kindling fire.

Sabbath violation may seem trivial in our eyes but it was extremely serious in YHWH's eyes! Perhaps, the question itself is problematic to begin with as R. Harrison states: "To categorize the transgression as 'minor' is to misunderstand the nature of sin. The so-called little white lie is just as much sin in the sight of God as is murder, for both are violations of Decalogue law" (*Numbers* 228). However, it is more likely that the severe penalty is because Sabbath violation entailed breach of the covenant (cf. Exod. 31:12-17). Longman considers the Sabbath "the pinnacle of the law during the Old Testament period" (137).

The story is comparable to Lev. 24:10-23 and Num. 9:6-12 in which YHWH has to give the verdict on the situation at hand and this becomes applicable to identical future situations. Hence, Num. 15:32-36 passes the law, as it were, that gathering wood on the Sabbath is liable of capital punishment (cf. Noth, *Numbers* 117). In short, gathering wood on the Sabbath is equivalent to making fire; as such it is a violation of the Sabbath, and hence the perpetrator should be executed. With this narrative, the author attempts to show in essence that the perpetrator's action is to be seen as an intentional ("high-handed") violation of the law even though Moses and the Israelites were not sure about it and needed to inquire of the Lord.

Message

In the final analysis, the story shows the seriousness of Sabbath violation which occurs when one works on the day. Sabbath is observed by refraining from work. Some, however, hold that worship was necessary (e.g., Watson 432); but the text simply shows that the Sabbath was violated by working on it, and hence, the perpetrator was executed. Wolff is correct on the passage: "Here let us especially note the fact that not even the slightest cultic activity is required to sanctify the sabbath. It is hallowed by doing exactly nothing, by resting" (504-05).

Jeremiah 17:19-27

The passage is often considered C material[12] and postexilic. There are several reasons for believing it to be postexilic. Some say that the words could not have come from Jeremiah because they hear a different voice in the text's support of the Sabbath as opposed to the prophet's supposed authentic voice against cult and rites (3:16, 6:20, 7:14, 21-22, 11:15, 14:12) (e.g., Calkins 161 n. 4; cf. Hyatt and Hopper 958-59). However, Jeremiah and other prophets did not oppose the cult and religious practices per se; they opposed the illegitimate or mere outward observance of the same (cf. Feinberg 489; Kidner 75 n. 91; Green 102-03). Others find here the postexilic Judaism's emphasis on the Sabbath (e.g., McKane 419). While it is true that the Sabbath, along with circumcision and dietary law, became a primary identifying marker of Jewish people in the exilic and postexilic periods, it was crucial even in the pre-exilic period (cf. Thompson, *Jeremiah* 429-30). After all, it was considered the sign of the covenant and found place in the Decalogue; its breach was punishable by death. Some believe that the fathers who had suffered exile because of their failure to keep the Sabbath are now presented as an example to warn their postexilic descendants (e.g., Carroll 367-69). Those who perceive the text to be postexilic consider vv. 25-26 as a hope of restoration, whereas the text is most likely referring to the continuation of the situation existent at the time of the oracle in the pre-exilic period (so also Lundbom 807). Yet others hold that Jeremiah's message was developed later by his follower or a redactor (e.g., Blackwood 149-50; cf. Thompson, *Jeremiah* 428-29; Bright, *Jeremiah* 120). Gladson, on the other hand, is agnostic and says that the issue of the text's origin "must be left open" (34-35). In the final analysis, however, there is nothing that would make it impossible for the words to have come from Jeremiah's mouth and hence be pre-exilic (see Huey 178; Craigie, Kelley, and Drinkard 238-39). In fact, Lundbom considers the oracle one of Jeremiah's earliest to be dated not long after 622 BCE (803-04, 808-09). Some others date it during Jehoiakim's reign (e.g., Green 103). The belief that the text must be postexilic is influenced, beside other reasons, by its striking resemblance with Neh. 13:15-22 (e.g., Holladay, *Jeremiah 1*, 509; McKane 417-18). However, this does not necessitate that the text be postexilic. Market economy prevailed in Jeremiah's time as well. In fact, Amos 8:5, which is accepted as pre-exilic and before Jeremiah's time, shows that the market economy was flourishing at the time and the traders saw the Sabbath as hindering their business. In addition, Nehemiah could have depended upon Jeremiah.

The pericope is a complete unit; it is introduced by כֹּה־אָמַר יְהֹוָה. The beginning of another section in 18:1 is indicated by a variation of the messenger formula הַדָּבָר אֲשֶׁר הָיָה אֶל־יִרְמְיָהוּ מֵאֵת יְהֹוָה לֵאמֹר. The passage has a simple oracular structure (cf. Thompson, *Jeremiah* 427): introduction (vv. 19-20), the law/command (vv. 21-23), blessing for obedience (vv. 24-26), and curse for disobedience (v. 27).

Message

The passage is clearly concerned with the observance of the Sabbath. The Sabbath is so important that its proper observance will mean continuation of the blessings while disregarding it will mean disaster or destruction; the fire here is most probably referring to the kind that the victors kindle in the aftermath of the war (cf. Craigie, Kelley, and Drinkard 239). In essence, then, it is pointing toward foreign invasion and destruction.

The message from YHWH is for all the people—kings, all Judah and Jerusalem (v. 20)—and it is to be proclaimed in all the gates of Jerusalem (v. 19). Sabbath observance is so crucial that it is a life-or-death issue: הִשָּׁמְרוּ בְּנַפְשׁוֹתֵיכֶם ("Take heed for the sake of your lives," v. 21). The fact is also clear from the apodoses (vv. 25-26, 27b). The ancestors did not keep the Sabbath but rebelled (v. 23).[13] The present generation is warned in the following verses to not follow their lead. If they obey and observe the Sabbath, blessings will follow (vv. 24-26) in the form of the continuation of (1) the throne with Davidic king, (2) the city of Jerusalem with its inhabitants, and (3) the temple with its cult. These three were fundamental to the life and religion of YHWH's people (so also Thompson, *Jeremiah* 431). On the contrary, if they disobey, then YHWH will send fire that will destroy everything (v. 27). Sabbath observance is a serious matter in YHWH's sight! The context of chapter 17 suggests that Sabbath violation is comparable to idolatry (vv. 1-4) as both cause fire to be kindled by YHWH (Carroll 367-68). Can Sabbath be more serious?

Sabbath Requirement

How then is the Sabbath to be observed? The answer is twofold: (1) by not bearing a burden on the day,[14] and (2) by not doing any work on it. The first is mentioned thrice (vv. 21-22, 24, 27) and the second twice (vv. 22, 24). The repetitions show how important these requirements are. There is essentially one requirement, i.e., to do no work on the day; carrying no burden is, in essence, an application of the "no work" command to a particular situation at hand (cf. Thompson, *Jeremiah* 429). The positive requirement is to keep the Sabbath holy, which also is mentioned thrice (vv. 22, 24, 27). Interestingly, in all the three instances the sanctifying of the Sabbath is mentioned in the same breath with the prohibition of work. What is one to make of it? The Sabbath is kept holy by refraining from work (more below). Also noteworthy is that there is no mention of worship in the text. Nonetheless, some struggle to accept the fact. For instance, to Ball the cessation of work as the only requirement of the Sabbath would entail "negative character" and an "enforced idleness." He believes that Jer. 17:19-27 *proves* "the Sabbath was a day of worship." He bases this conclusion on two grounds: (1) the Sabbath is to be hallowed, and (2) the promise of bountiful sacrifices-offerings at the temple if the Sabbath is observed (v. 26) refers to the "celebration of the Sabbath festival" (Ball 101). Regarding the sanctifying of the Sabbath, we shall have time to discuss below. The promise of abundant offerings, however, is not with reference to the Sabbath but the continuation of the temple cult in general. There is no cultic (or worship) requirement in the text. We need to have a proper theology of rest and avoid seeing it as an "enforced idleness."

Nehemiah 10:31a[32a]; 13:15-22a

These texts give a postexilic scenario of Sabbath enforcement. The situation is not very different from the pre-exilic situation encountered by Jeremiah (17:19-27; cf. Amos 8:5). The problem is the defilement of the Sabbath particularly by trading on it.

Text and Meaning

Many scholars believe 13:15-22 precedes 10:31.[15] The suggestion is understandable because it seems more logical for Nehemiah to have acted in bringing renewal after seeing the law broken. The reverse, however, is probably the case as Eskenazi also asserts: "The arrangement in Ezra-Nehemiah ascribes the reforms to the community as a whole, making Nehemiah's activities essentially the administering of communally ordained regulations" (124-25). Moreover, Nehemiah's actions of closing the gates and placing guards plus prohibiting the traders from lodging outside the wall in chapter 13 makes more sense in the event of the Jews' non-compliance to the commitment they had made earlier in 10:31. In all likelihood, the first attempt involved motivating the inhabitants of Jerusalem to avoid buying on the Sabbath even though the vendors were in operation (10:31); this happened during Nehemiah's first term as the governor (see Neh. 5:14). On his return after a visit to Babylon (Neh. 13:6-7), Nehemiah found that things had changed and even worsened. Thus, in a subsequent attempt, he had to prevent even the vendors from showing up (13:15-22).

Many believe 10:31 extends the prohibited works on the Sabbath to include buying; selling was already prohibited (Amos 8:5; Jer. 17:19-27) (e.g., Clines, "Nehemiah 10" 113, 114-15).[16] This is probably correct. Moreover, while most consider the vav of וּבְיוֹם in the phrase בַּשַּׁבָּת וּבְיוֹם קֹדֶשׁ to be conjunctive (thus, 'on the Sabbath or on a holy day'), Fensham (240) takes it to be explicative (thus, 'on the Sabbath, the holy day'). The latter implies that the reference here is to the Sabbath alone and does not include other holy days. In any case, the Sabbath day is included.

Neh. 13:15-22 has a beautiful structure with a major crisis and its resolution; within this broader framework, there are three crises and accompanying resolutions. The structure is akin to three scenes of a play that together form the mega scene.

Crisis: Widespread Sabbath violation (vv. 15-16)

  Resolution: Temporary and permanent measures to stop the violation (vv. 17-22a)

    Crisis 1: Treading and trading (15a)

      Resolution 1: Warning to stop (15b)

    Crisis 2: Foreigners selling merchandise (16)

      Resolution 2: Leaders rebuked and gates secured (17-19)

    Crisis 3: Traders attempt to defy (20)

      Resolution 3: Warning including threat of using force (21)

Nehemiah sees a widespread violation of the Sabbath and takes steps to stop it. The violation involved working—treading winepresses, transporting merchandise, and trading (vv. 15-16). The vendors could have been non-Israelites alone (v. 16), which is conceivable in the light of 10:31. The latter verse suggests that the vendors were non-Israelites; YHWH's people were only involved in buying. However, it is also possible that in chapter 13 the vendors included Israelites as well (v. 15). If this is correct, then the vow the people made in 10:31 is not only neglected, but the Sabbath violation has worsened as it now includes selling in addition to buying. In any event, YHWH's people had violated the Sabbath.

Nehemiah begins consecration of the Sabbath by reproving the leaders (v. 17). The likely reason is that they did nothing to prevent the Sabbath violation. In addition, they themselves could have also been involved in the violation. In any case, they were responsible as leaders. Profaning the Sabbath is evil thing (הַדָּבָר הָרָע), says Nehemiah. Moreover, he perceives the destruction of Jerusalem and the exile as a consequence of Sabbath violation (v. 18a) presumably because it represented a breach of the covenant. He probably sees in them the fulfillment of Jeremiah's prophecy (Jer. 17:19-27; cf. Ezek. 20:12-24), which in turn is based on Pentateuchal Sabbath law (cf. Fishbane 132). Rhetorical question(s) is used to make this assertion. Nehemiah is certain that the current state of Sabbath desecration increases divine wrath: וְאַתֶּם מוֹסִיפִים חָרוֹן עַל־יִשְׂרָאֵל לְחַלֵּל אֶת־הַשַּׁבָּת ("Yet you are adding wrath on Israel by profaning the Sabbath," v. 18b). He thus takes stern measures to prevent Sabbath desecration (vv. 19-22a).

The first part of v. 19 is obscure (see H. Williamson, *Ezra-Nehemiah*, WBC 393 n. 19a) but the overall meaning of the verse is clear. Nehemiah orders the gates of the city closed as the dusk approaches on the sixth day and they are to be opened only after the Sabbath is over. In addition, he stations his men at the gates to prevent goods from being brought into the city. Later he mobilizes the Levites to do the job (v. 22a). Although the Levites were responsible for guarding the temple gates and not the city gates, Nehemiah extends their work as the latter too was construed as a sacred task since it involved preserving the sanctity of the Sabbath; this is also the reason they were asked to purify themselves before taking up their guard (Blenkinsopp, *Ezra-Nehemiah* 361; cf. Clines, *Ezra* 245; Breneman 273). The use of Nehemiah's men was a temporary arrangement at the moment of crisis and then the Levites were mobilized as the permanent measure to ensure the continuity of the new situation following the crisis (see H. Williamson, *Ezra-Nehemiah*, WBC 396; Klein 848; Fensham 264-65; Blenkinsopp, *Ezra-Nehemiah* 361; Campbell 116). Myers writes: "Levitical guards were required because they could be consecrated for Sabbath duty, a requirement that could not be met by laymen" (216). The argument seems erroneous because initially the laymen—Nehemiah's men—were mobilized, which seems to suggest that laymen would be qualified for the job. The use of the Levites is probably due to four reasons. First, they were readily available. Second, they were permanently available. Third, YHWH had set them apart for "holy tasks," and as mentioned above, the task at hand was construed as sacred. Fourth, in line with the third reason, giving the task a sacred outlook would make it more forceful on the general populace.

When the gates were closed and guards stationed, the traders spent the night outside the wall on a few Sabbaths (v. 20). The reason could be, as Breneman (273) believes, to gain an edge over other vendors once the market resumed after the Sabbath. However, it is more likely that this was done in order to either attempt sneaking in the merchandise into the city or to sell to the city-dwellers walking in and out of the city, possibly through some postern gate (Blenkinsopp, *Ezra-Nehemiah* 361). That such is probably the case is supported by Nehemiah's response; he found it problematic and threatened to use force (יָד אֶשְׁלַח בָּכֶם, "I will lay hand on you") to stop them if they continued their act (v. 21a). As the governor, he had the power and authority to do so. Nehemiah presumably saw malintention in the vendors' act: an attempt at smuggling or a temptation to the city-dwellers to break the Sabbath. Nehemiah's threat worked; the sellers stopped bringing merchandise and lodging outside the wall on the Sabbath (v. 21b).

Message
Nehemiah's beliefs about Sabbath violation (vv. 17-18) and his stern actions to prevent it (vv. 19-22a) show that Sabbath observation is a serious matter. What, then, can we learn about the Sabbath from this text? The message of the passage, in short,

is: work (here treading, portering, and trading) profanes the
Sabbath day and hence it should be prohibited at any cost. There
is no mention of worship/cult. Brown, however, comments
on the passage: "Israelites from the surrounding towns and
villages were no longer visiting the 'holy city' to worship on
the Sabbath but to attend the city's busy markets, in order to
buy and sell their produce up and down its crowded streets"
(*Nehemiah* 237). Later he describes the Sabbath as providing
"opportunity for spiritual worship and physical relaxation"
(ibid. 240); one wonders what "spiritual worship" means. Shao
and Shao comment: "Whereas the Sabbath is a day of rest,
related to the creation of God, it should be a day of worship
(Exod 20:8-11)" (232). Neither Brown nor the Shaos give any
explanation as to how worship was to be enacted. The text says
nothing about worship; rather it addresses only the necessity
of refraining from work. In fact, v. 22a is very clear that in
this case consecrating the Sabbath meant guarding the gates
so that trade can be prevented because this was desecrating
the Sabbath; there is no indication of worship.

וָאֹמְרָה לַלְוִיִּם אֲשֶׁר יִהְיוּ מִטַּהֲרִים וּבָאִים שֹׁמְרִים הַשְּׁעָרִים לְקַדֵּשׁ אֶת־יוֹם הַשַּׁבָּת

And I commanded the Levites that they should purify themselves
and come [and] guard the gates to consecrate the day of the
Sabbath (v. 22a).

Leviticus 23:3

Lev. 23:3 is usually taken by commentators to say that the
Sabbath involved communal assembly, primarily because
מִקְרָא־קֹדֶשׁ is juxtaposed to the Sabbath. Gerstenberger,
however, takes this verse to refer to the seven Sabbaths in
relation to the religious festivals explained in the following
verses of the chapter and not to the weekly Sabbath (341). The
proposal is noteworthy given the context of the chapter, that of

providing the stipulations for major Israelite festivals. However, the statement 'six days shall work be done' poses a problem because it clearly suggests that v. 3 is referring to the weekly Sabbath. Gerstenberger acknowledges the difficulty but brushes it aside quickly without providing satisfactory explanation (see 341). The reference indeed is to the weekly Sabbath.

The problem lies in the understanding of the phrase מִקְרָא־קֹדֶשׁ, usually translated 'a sacred assembly' or 'a holy convocation.'[17] The translation, which is likely a misunderstanding of the phrase, has contributed to a large extent toward the understanding that the Sabbath was a day of worship, precisely a day of communal assembly. Thus, the translations along the line of 'sacred assembly,' despite their predominance, are likely mistranslations. Some translate it differently; for example, "a sacred occasion" (Levine, *Leviticus* 155; Milgrom, *Leviticus 23-27*, 1932; TNK), "a holy time" (Gerstenberger 334), "proclaimed holiness" (Knohl 74), and "a proclamation of holiness" (Kiuchi 413). One thing noteworthy in these translations is that they avoid the commonly used "assembly/convocation"; as such, they are better translations. They do not miscommunicate giving the readers the mistaken idea that the weekly Sabbath involved communal gathering.

Out of the twenty-two occurrences of מִקְרָא in the Bible, eighteen times it appears in the phrase מִקְרָא־קֹדֶשׁ (Morgenstern 314). Morgenstern argues that מִקְרָא never meant 'assembly' (314-17; cf. Andreasen 58-59).[18] He further contends that מִקְרָא־קֹדֶשׁ does not mean sacred assembly but "a proclamation of holiness" or "proclamation of a taboo"; the Sabbath was a taboo day in which abstention from work was necessary and no religious activity was required (Morgenstern 314-20). The view that it was a taboo day is based on the prohibition of work, but this is problematic. The Bible portrays the abstention of work on the Sabbath as a gift of God, a welcome day of rest rather than a taboo day. Moreover, קֹדֶשׁmeans "holiness/sacredness," not "taboo." However, his conclusion that מִקְרָא־קֹדֶשׁ did not mean sacred assembly is correct. First, מִקְרָאmost probably did not mean assembly (see also Kiuchi 415, 420). Second, if 'sacred assembly' was the intent of the author/redactor,קָדוֹשׁ (adjective) would have been a better choice than קֹדֶשׁalthough the latter can be used adjectivally (cf. Morgenstern 316). Translations such as "sacred assembly," "sacred occasion," and "holy time" take קֹדֶשׁ to be adjectival, whereas "proclaimed holiness" (Knohl) takes מִקְרָא to be adjectival. However, in light of the fact that both מִקְרָא andקֹדֶשׁ are nouns in a construct relationship, it is better to translate them likewise. Hence, the best translation of the phrase is "a proclamation of holiness" (e.g., Kiuchi 413). Third, if 'sacred assembly' were intended, there are words which unambiguously mean "assembly" and can be used to refer to the assemblies of religious character as well, yet they are not used here, e.g., קָהָל (1 Kgs 8:14; 1 Chron. 29:20) and עֵדָה (1 Kgs 8:5). All these point to the conclusion that there is no reference to an assembly—a communal gathering—in the phrase מִקְרָא־קֹדֶשׁ. Old Testament scholarship has erroneously accepted the now near-consensus translation "sacred assembly" or the like. For instance, Wenham translates the phrase as "holy convention" and states that putting some "scraps of information together" shows that it "was a national gathering for public worship" (*Leviticus* 301). Block, however, concurs with us that the translations of the phrase akin to 'sacred/holy assembly/convocation' are misleading because they give the idea that there was corporate gathering for worship. He translates the Hebrew phrase as "holy proclamation" and sees the possibility of shofars (ram's horns) blown in villages and towns at sunset on the sixth day that "would not summon people to assemble for worship, but simply signal that all work should cease" (Block, *For the Glory* 276-77). There seems to be a give-and-take to the misunderstanding, i.e., the assumption that the Sabbath involved cult/assembly led to translating מִקְרָא־קֹדֶשׁ as 'sacred assembly' and this translation in turn strengthened the view that the Sabbath involved cult/assembly.

Although Morgenstern's view that the term מִקְרָא is of late postexilic origin (314, 316) is dubitable, it is quite probable that מִקְרָא־קֹדֶשׁ received "the altogether secondary and unetymological meaning" or the "false interpretation" akin to 'sacred assembly' only after the practice of assembling began with the development of the synagogues (see Morgenstern 318-19). On its own, the phrase has nothing to do with assembly (or worship). Moreover, no prescription is given in the passage as to how the worship or assembly is to be carried out. The translation "a proclamation of holiness," remaining faithful to the Hebrew, conveys simply that the Sabbath is a "holy" day,[19] on which there is no debate.

Another phrase which appears in this verse that too has somewhat contributed to the (mis)understanding of the Sabbath as a day of worship is שַׁבַּת שַׁבָּתוֹן. Many translate the phrase "a Sabbath of solemn rest" (e.g., ESV, NKJV; Kiuchi 413; Wenham, *Leviticus* 297). The word "solemn" often has religious overtones which, in the legal and/or festal context of the OT, can give the idea of cultic activity. The misunderstanding is heightened by its juxtaposition with מִקְרָא־קֹדֶשׁ which as argued has usually been mistranslated; שַׁבַּת שַׁבָּתוֹן and מִקְרָא־קֹדֶשׁ are in apposition in the verse. שַׁבַּת שַׁבָּתוֹן is a superlative construction; thus the phrase is better translated "a Sabbath

of compete rest/cessation" or "a rest of complete resting."
Gane's translation is interesting, i.e., "sabbathly sabbath" or
"super-Sabbath" (388). Levine captures the idea with the phrase
"the most restful cessation" (*Leviticus* 155; also W. Kaiser,
"Leviticus" 1157).[20] Milgrom does the same with "the most
restful rest" (*Leviticus 23-27*, 1959). The idea is that the day
involves complete cessation of work and hence an absolute
rest. According to Milgrom, only שַׁבַּת שַׁבָּתוֹן involved "a
total cessation of labor" (כָּל־מְלָאכָה, "all work"), while other
holidays involved only cessation of מְלָאכֶת עֲבֹדָה, "laborious
work" (*Numbers* 409; cf. Hartley 375). There is probably a
difference between the Sabbaths related to the festivals (see
Lev. 23) in which people cease from work in order to celebrate
the festival and the שַׁבַּת שַׁבָּתוֹן in which rest itself is the goal
of the cessation (Levine, *Leviticus* 155). In any case, the phrase
is better translated without "solemn"; the word is somewhat
obscure, possibly misleading, and simply unnecessary.

One more phrase that should not be overlooked in this
verse is בְּכֹל מוֹשְׁבֹתֵיכֶם ('in all your settlements/dwelling
places'). Kiuchi is correct that the phrase shows "the sabbath
is thus the day on which the Lord is willing to meet the people,
not by their going to the sanctuary, but in their own settlements"
(421, emphasis mine; cf. Levine, *Leviticus* 155). Thus, contra
Wenham, the Sabbath did not involve "national gathering for
public worship"; it was to be celebrated by the Israelites not at
the sanctuary or at a common place of assembly but in their
own residences. Priests, however, were involved in the cult at
the sanctuary. In the final analysis, Lev. 23:3 does not support
the theory that the Sabbath was a day of worship—cult or
assembly—for non-priestly Israelites.

Structurally, too, Lev. 23:3 shows that the primary concern of the Sabbath is not worship but rest as opposed to work on six days:[21]

A Six days

  B shall work be done,

    C but the seventh day is a Sabbath of complete rest, a proclamation of holiness.

  B' You shall do no work;

    A' it is a Sabbath to/of YHWH in all your dwelling places.

שַׁבָּת שַׁבָּתוֹן and מִקְרָא־קֹדֶשׁ (C) are bracketed by work/no-work concern, which strengthens the argument that the day is concerned with the issue of work, not worship.

In addition, it should also be noted that the weekly Sabbath has influenced the major festivals of Israel and hence there are Sabbaths even in the midst of the national celebrations that are accompanied by communal cultic/worship activities (Lev. 23:4ff). The influence is from the weekly Sabbath to the "festive Sabbaths" and not vice versa. Therefore, the festive Sabbaths are days of rest or cessation from work, but the weekly Sabbath is not a day of communal gathering for worship.

Hosea 2:11[13]; Isaiah 1:13

Hos. 2:11 and Isa. 1:13 are sometimes cited to suggest that the Sabbath involved assembly and/or cult.[22] However, at a closer investigation, such is not the case. Let us first look at Hos. 2:11.

וְהִשְׁבַּתִּי כָּל־מְשׂוֹשָׂהּ חַגָּהּ חָדְשָׁהּ וְשַׁבַּתָּהּ וְכֹל מוֹעֲדָהּ

And I will cause to end all her rejoicing—her festivals, her new moons, and her Sabbaths—and all her appointed times.[23]

There is nothing in the verse that suggests the Sabbath involved worship. The verse simply asserts that YHWH is going to end Israel's times of rejoicing, its appointed occasions. The occasions mentioned are in the ascending order of occurrence: 'festivals' refers most likely to the three yearly pilgrim festivals, new moon is a monthly phenomenon, and Sabbath a weekly one (see Andersen and Freedman 250; Wood 177; Andreasen 61). There is a tendency to think of the Sabbath as not being joyful but a burden because of the restrictions. The Pharisaic and Rabbinic traditions attest that such could happen, but the Scripture tells us that it was to be a welcome day of rest from labor; hence a day of rejoicing (cf. Isa. 58:13-14).

Some take the whole of חַגָּה חָדְשָׁהּ וְשַׁבַּתָּהּ וְכֹל מֹועֲדָהּ to be an explication of כָּל־מְשֹׂושָׂהּ (e.g., Andreasen 61), while others consider only חַגָּהּ חָדְשָׁהּ וְשַׁבַּתָּהּ to be explicative of כָּל־מְשֹׂושָׂהּ and וְכֹל מֹועֲדָהּ to be parallel to it (e.g., Stuart, Hosea-Jonah 43).[24] Both are valid, and in either case, the message is clear: God will put an end to all the occasions of Israelite celebrations—yearly, monthly, and weekly—likely because they had turned them into Baal worship or festivals for Baal and had forgotten YHWH (v. 13). The confusion that the Sabbath was a day of corporate worship is often the result of translating מֹועֵד as 'assemblies' (e.g., Mays 35; Andersen and Freedman 5, 250; Laetsch 27, "festival gatherings"). We have translated מֹועֵד as "appointed times."[25] Andreasen rightly says that "we learn nothing about the way in which these occasions were celebrated" from this verse (61). We cannot conclude from Hos. 2:11 that the Sabbath entailed assembly, cult, or public worship; all we can say is that it was one of Israel's joyous occasions. As such, it was probably celebrated at their homes (Lev. 23:3) and did not involve communal gathering.

We now turn to Isa. 1:13.

חֹדֶשׁ וְשַׁבָּת קְרֹא מִקְרָא לֹא־אוּכַל אָוֶן וַעֲצָרָה

New moons and Sabbaths, proclaiming of festivals; I cannot bear
iniquities and festivities (v. 13b).[26]

Some take קְרֹא מִקְרָא to be in apposition to חֹדֶשׁ וְשַׁבָּת (e.g.,
Andreasen 59), which is possible because there is no vav with
קְרֹא; some others translate as though there were one (e.g.,
NRSV).[27] In any case, the verse does not show that the Sabbath
entailed communal assembly. The problem is with translating
מִקְרָא as assembly. Andreasen, drawing upon several others,
has shown that מִקְרָא here should be taken to mean festival
or feast but not assembly (58-59). This is in line with what
we have argued previously. Thus, this construction does not
prove that the Sabbath involved assembly. עֲצָרָה can refer to
assembly (2 Chron. 7:9) but is not limited to this meaning,
particularly in light of the meaning of the root verb that it
comes from, i.e., עצר (see Wright and Milgrom 310-15). The
overall context here (vv. 10-17) suggests that the word has a
broader nuance. Hence, we translate it "festivities" (O. Kaiser
24 translates "festivals"). Oswalt is probably correct that אָוֶן
and וַעֲצָרָה form a hendiadys (*Isaiah 1-39*, 97). In any case, it
is the intermingling of piety with iniquity that God detests.
As Oswalt puts it: "What God cannot bear is 'religious sin'"
(*Isaiah 1-39*, 97). The point of the verse, then, is that YHWH
hates Israel's celebrations (cf. Hos. 2:11) because they are filled
with iniquity.

The overall context (vv. 10-17) shows that the problem
here is Israel's illegitimate celebration of its appointed occasions,
whether cultic or non-cultic; v. 15 even mentions prayer
(תְּפִלָּה). The cult is certainly in view (vv. 11-13) but the

reference is to the cult in general, which likely includes the cult that priests were involved in on the Sabbath. The verse says nothing about whether or not the non-priestly Israelites were involved in some cult or assembly on the Sabbath.

Isaiah 66:23; Ezekiel 46:1-5

Isaiah 66:23 does mention worship or bowing down (חוה) on the Sabbath. There seems to be a consensus among critical scholars today that Isa. 40-66 is late material (exilic/postexilic).[28] Accordingly, Isa. 56-66 is exilic (e.g., McCullough 27-35) or postexilic (e.g., Nickelsburg 581; Leclerc 132; Chan 449-52). However, there are strong voices that contend for a pre-exilic dating of the chapters (e.g., Rooker, "Dating Isaiah 40-66" 303-12). In any case, Isa. 66:23 is undoubtedly eschatological (see Childs, *Isaiah* 542; Blenkinsopp, *Isaiah 56-66*, 316; Grogan 348). The eschatological expectation, among other things, is that all nations (כָל־בָּשָׂר) will come to worship YHWH.[29] The immediate context (vv. 18-24) shows that the text is eschatological. The fulfillment of this eschatological hope (or prophecy) is a matter of debate. Some see it metaphorically and consider it fulfilled in the Incarnation. For instance, Hailey believes that with the coming of Christ, the new order has commenced and the old Israelite order has been abolished.[30] In this schema, there is no place for new moons or Sabbaths. Oswalt, too, takes it symbolically and comments on v. 23:

> This is obviously symbolic language, since the possibility of people from all over a world like ours traveling back and forth to Jerusalem every week is ludicrous. But what is being symbolized is anything but ludicrous. The prophet envisions a day when the Spirit of God makes his home in every heart and where every heart is Jerusalem (*Isaiah 40-66*, 692).

Others believe that this hope will be fulfilled after the second coming of Christ (e.g., Grogan 15; cf. Youngblood 170). Yet others see the possibility of its fulfillment encompassing both the first and second advents of Christ (e.g., Motyer 540). Taken at face value, however, we should also allow for the possibility that the prophet envisages worship of YHWH at the Jerusalem temple in which gentiles (כָל־בָּשָׂר) too will join. The word לְפָנַי ("in my presence") in this context is likely a reference to the temple, YHWH's abode. In that case, if the text is postexilic, then this was expected sometime in the farther future; if it is pre-exilic, then one might contend that the prophecy was fulfilled after the return from the Babylonian exile. However, the heightened expectations of the text were not fulfilled even after the return. Hence, if literal, then its fulfillment must lie in a distant future; it did not find fruition in the OT period. Unger believes in the literal fulfillment of the prophecy following Christ's return in that the Sabbath which has now been suspended due to Israel's infidelity will be reinstated (58-59). There is an underlying belief in the millennial reign of Christ following His return in Unger's view (cf. Criswell 303-09), which in turn is a highly debated issue. The many interpretations should caution us against basing our theology of the Sabbath on this obscure text whose interpretation is no easy matter. Is the prophecy to be interpreted literally or symbolically? The latter approach far outweighs the former in Christian scholarship. Moreover, do v. 22 (new heavens and new earth) and v. 23 (observance of new moon and Sabbath by all flesh) envision fulfillment of different types (literal vs. symbolic) and times (cf. millennial interpretation, e.g., there will be literal restoration of Jewish temple and cult in the millennial kingdom, and new heavens and new earth will follow the completion of that kingdom)? When, and more importantly, how the prophet's words will be (or was) fulfilled is dubious.

Likewise, Ezek. 46:1-5 gives prescriptions for worship at the temple on the Sabbaths (and new moons) by the prince (נָשִׂיא) and the people of the land (עַם־הָאָרֶץ). The prince shall offer sacrifices and bow down (חוה) before YHWH (v. 2), and the people also shall bow down (v. 3). No prescription is given for the people to offer sacrifices. Either it is not required or those offered by the prince also represent the people (cf. Ezek. 45:13-18; Zimmerli 493). In any case, this is a clear reference to worship. The text is prophetic; it is expecting such a situation in the future. The practice prevalent in the time of its writing is not reflected here. Some believe the text to be postexilic (Robinson, *Origin* 207-09), while others argue for an exilic dating (e.g., Duguid 25). How far in the future is the prophet looking? The text is clearly eschatological. Alexander believes that the Sabbath and the new moon celebrations will be observed in the millennial kingdom when the Mosaic covenant will be reinstituted and fulfilled (986; so also Cooper 402-03; contra Block, *Ezekiel 25-48*, 677). If the text is exilic and expects its literal fulfillment in the near future, i.e., in the second temple, that did not happen. There was no prince—obviously referring to a king, and most likely, a Davidic king—in the postexilic Israel. Moreover, the scenario envisaged by Ezek. 40-48 was not realized either (cf. Duguid 522). The fulfillment, if literal, has to be in the distant future. However, like the Isaiah text above, there are some who interpret the text symbolically. For instance, Duguid takes chapters 40-48 symbolically and identifies the temple with Jesus, i.e., the whole vision is fulfilled in Christ (522-26). There are yet others who see double fulfillment. For instance, C. Wright believes in "several layers of significance to the temple vision" with literal fulfillment in the aftermath of the exile, and a symbolic fulfillment in Christ's coming and thereafter (*Ezekiel* 343-44).

The difficulties faced in interpreting Isa. 66:23 are present in interpreting Ezek. 46:1-5 as well. Both are eschatological and one cannot be certain how these texts are to be understood. Do they envision literal fulfillment, symbolic fulfillment, or both? But for the millenarianists who believe in the restoration of the Jewish nation together with its temple, cult, and festivals in the Millennium,[31] Isa. 66:23 and Ezek. 46:1-5 are an enigma to the interpreters. The millennial interpretations, nonetheless, have their own problems (see Duguid 521-22).

In the final analysis, we need to be careful about basing our whole theology on a few eschatological texts whose interpretation is a conundrum when there are plenty of other texts that speak unambiguously on the subject. The challenge of interpreting OT eschatological texts needs no elucidation (see Petersen, "Eschatology" 575-79; Ladd 130-33). This fact is also evident from our study. In short, neither Isa. 66:23 nor Ezek. 46:1-5 attests that the Sabbath involved corporate worship. None of these texts reflect the Sabbath practice prevalent in the days of the prophets who spoke them.

Interestingly, Ezek. 46:1 designates the non-Sabbath days as שֵׁשֶׁת יְמֵי הַמַּעֲשֶׂה ('the six working days' a hapax legomenon), which implies that the Sabbath is 'the one non-working (resting) day.' The phrase, thus, expresses the primary concern of the Sabbath, i.e., rest or cessation from work. The significance is heightened because the phrase appears in the context dominated by cult in the future temple (literal or symbolic!).

Keeping the Sabbath Holy

Another major reason for believing that the Sabbath involved worship is the fact that Sabbath is associated with holiness, e.g., "keep the Sabbath holy" (Exod. 20:8; Deut. 5:12). The assumption is that if it is to be kept holy, then there needs to be some "holy" activity, namely, cult or sacred assembly, some worship *activity*. For instance, Ross states, "This day of rest was a time of physical refreshment to be sure, but the instructions to make the day holy reveal a greater purpose than simply regathering strength for another week. The day was set aside for worship and spiritual service and was not given over to personal pursuits" (399-400). Ross is correct that the day was not to be spent on "personal pursuits"; the law required cessation from work. However, he provides no explanation for the nature of worship or the meaning of "spiritual service" for which he says the day was set aside. He later writes, based on the phrase מִקְרָא־קֹדֶשׁ, "Each Sabbath was thus a sacred assembly. Exactly what happened when the people came together in the presence of the Lord is unclear, for no sacrifices or purification rites are instructed" (Ross 402). Perhaps by worship, Ross means sacred assembly; but we have shown that מִקְרָא־קֹדֶשׁ does not mean sacred assembly. Moreover, his admission that what happened at the sacred assembly is unknown because no instructions are given for the same, is crucial. Would one not expect some instruction if such assembly was required since Sabbath-keeping was such a serious matter that its violation could result in execution? No instruction is given because the Sabbath required no cultic or "worship" activity from the general populace. Bosman, while acknowledging the cultic engagement of the priests on the Sabbath, rightly states:

> OT interpretation has frequently presumed an *unfortunate equivalence*
> between the Sabbath becoming a hallowed day set aside for God
> and a cultic observance peculiar to the Sabbath. It is therefore
> important to appreciate the theological significance of ordinary
> Israelites abstaining from work without resorting to any cultic
> festivity reserved for the Sabbath (1160, emphasis mine).

The priests were involved in sacrifices on the weekdays as well;
the difference is that the Sabbath required additional sacrifices
and changing of loaves in the sanctuary (Lev. 24:5-8). Jenson,
too, has highlighted well the "non-cultic character" of the
Sabbath (see 195-96).

If the Sabbath did not involve cult or assembly, what then
does it mean to keep the Sabbath holy? Holiness in the Bible
has the idea of set-apartness. Thus, Lundbom can write, "To
keep the Sabbath day holy is to keep it 'set apart' from other
days" (806). This hallowing is done by desisting from work,
which sets the day apart from other days (six workdays). Nelson
holds that the Sabbath is likely holy intrinsically because of its
association with YHWH. He adds, "However, Israel also marks
Sabbath off as holy by nonnormal human behavior, that is, by
not working" (Nelson 82). Cessation from work sets the day
apart from common use and gives it a sacred character. Wolff
notes that God sanctified the Sabbath by setting it apart from
the workdays (502). According to Lundbom, "The Sabbath
must not be treated like any other day; it is a sacred day set
aside for rest" (808). Indeed, a day set aside for rest, not for
cult or assembly!

For the Sabbath to be holy, cultic activity is not a must. The
assertion is also strengthened by the fact that the animals, too,
are listed among those to be allowed rest. By extension, in the
sabbatical year even the land is to observe Sabbath (Lev. 25).

Rest is central to the Sabbath.[32] Brueggemann, commenting on the Sabbath, concurs: "There is no mention of worship. The way in which this day is to be acknowledged as holy—i.e., different and special—is to separate it from all days of required activity, productivity, coercive performance, self-securing, or service to other human agents" ("Exodus" 845). How is the Sabbath consecrated or kept holy? By desisting from work, i.e., by resting (cf. Wolff 499). The problem is in associating worship with some cultic or religious *activity*. For many, the underlying question is: How can non-activity be holy? I contend that the non-activity (i.e., rest) as an imitation of the Creator in obedience to His command with the acknowledgment that it is His gift to His people is in itself sacred.

Summary

We have studied several key passages covering the Sabbath from pre-Sinaitic times to the postexilic period. The unequivocal conclusion is that the Sabbath day did not involve worship—cult or religious assembly—for the non-priestly Israelites. Cult was limited to the priests at the temple. The phrases מִקְרָא־קֹדֶשׁ and שַׁבַּת שַׁבָּתוֹן in Lev. 23:3 lie behind the widely accepted assumption in biblical scholarship that the Sabbath involved "worship" for the general populace, which we have shown is erroneous. Hos. 2:11 and Isa. 1:13 are sometimes cited to suggest that the Sabbath involved assembly and/or cult, which we have seen is incorrect. Moreover, the command to consecrate the Sabbath is also behind the assumption; however, the Sabbath is consecrated not by some cultic or religious activity but by non-activity. The OT commandments and observances of the Sabbath did not involve communal worship. Isa. 66:23 and Ezek. 46:1-5 do mention worship on the Sabbath at the temple, but these are eschatological texts whose interpretation is a conundrum. One cannot be certain whether they are to be understood literally or symbolically or both. In addition, the time of their fulfillment is also unclear—after the return from the exile in the sixth century BCE, at the first coming of Christ, at His second coming, or there are multiple fulfillments at different times. All in all, no OT text ascertains that the Sabbath involved worship for non-priestly Israelites; rather every text is clear that rest or cessation of work is compulsory. In the words of Blomberg, "Indeed, if all we had were the Hebrew Scriptures we might never guess that a day of rest eventually also became a day for worship." The Sabbath became a day of worship in the STP (Blomberg, "Sabbath as Fulfilled," *Perspectives* 307; cf. ibid. 340, 353).

Endnotes

[1] The command does not mean that a person could not step outside the tent; other tasks such as attending to the livestock and relieving oneself required going out. The command was in essence a ban on going outside to gather manna (so Stuart, *Exodus* 383). The manna would not be available anyway as YHWH would provide none on the day.

[2] However, it is not impossible that the Israelites assembled at certain place other than the tabernacle prior to its construction. How else would Moses and Aaron have communicated to the people if there was no assemblage prior to the tabernacle's existence? Hence, although קִרְבוּ לִפְנֵי יְהוָה (קִרְבוּ) has a technical usage in the OT, the phrase could mean assembling elsewhere prior to the existence of the tabernacle, yet in the presence of YHWH (cf. Ferris 196-97). Likewise, it is not impossible that YHWH's glory would appear except at Sinai or the tabernacle (contra Baden). Verses 33-34, however, have clearer references to the tabernacle and the Ark.

[3] It is possible that the use of תּוֹרָה in the verse anticipates the giving of the law at Sinai; as such the test with manna could actually be, as it were, a "pretest" to see whether they would show positive signs of a people who would follow the Torah that was to be given in the near future (cf. Stuart, *Exodus* 372). However, it is probable that Moses used the word in its general sense, i.e., "instruction."

[4] Unless otherwise stated, the Scripture translations throughout this work are my own.

[5] However, we cannot deduce from the account that YHWH ceases all work on the Sabbaths; all we can say is that He refrained from providing manna on the day and this was probably done in order to enforce His command on the Israelites.

[6] There is also an acknowledgment that the juxtaposition of the Sabbath and the tabernacle highlights the sanctity of both time and space (e.g., Sarna 201). Likewise, the juxtaposition of the Sabbath and the sanctuary in some texts (Lev. 19:30, 26:2) is likely a command to revere the sanctity of both time (Sabbath) and space (sanctuary), and does not necessarily mean that the Sabbath involved cultic activity at the sanctuary for the Israelite community.

[7] Drawing primarily on Jer. 7:18, Robinson believes that "gathering wood" and "kindling fire" is one act associated with the worship of other gods, which is comparable to the "strange fire" offered by Nadab and Abihu in Lev. 10. Hence, he holds that the prohibition in Exod. 35:3 is fire associated with the worship of other gods/idols. Further, the original adjective זָרָה ("strange") could have been dropped by later redactor because (1) he did not understand the meaning of "strange fire" at a much later stage, and (2) he sought to expand the application of this cultic fire prohibition to include domestic fire as well—a postexilic development. Robinson thus believes the original statement of 35:3 to have been "You shall not kindle a *strange* fire in all your habitations." A late Priestly redactor 'sabbatized' the command by adding "on the Sabbath day" and deleting "strange" ("Strange Fire" 306-13). The theory is highly conjectural and lacks textual support (cf. Burnside 47 n. 5).

[8] That Enns and Stuart believe the Sabbath to be the day of worship for everyone is clear also from their application of the text. For example, "When the saints of God meet on Sunday mornings, they, like the Israelites before them, are worshiping in holy time and space. It is holy time because, like the Sabbath, it is the one day in seven set apart for worship. It is holy space in the sense that church buildings set apart from common use are dedicated to the worship of God" (Enns, 558; cf. Stuart, *Exodus* 654-55).

[9] See Ashley 291; Knierim and Coats 198, 201; R. D. Cole 254; Wenham, *Numbers* 131; Brown, *Numbers* 139.

[10] Weingreen 361-64. See Phillips' objection of Weingreen (Phillips, "Woodgatherer" 125-28; cf. Robinson, "Strange Fire" 301f). Phillips' view is not convincing either. He sees the Sabbath texts on the restriction of domestic fire as exilic and/or postexilic, and believes that Exod. 16:23, 35:3 and Num. 15:32-36 together extend the Sabbath restrictions to the domestic arena (ibid. 127).

[11] Note also his connection between gathering wood here with gathering straw for bricks in Egypt based on the use of the same verb (Burnside 54, 56, 60; cf. Novick 5).

[12] Mowinckel, building on Duhm's work, categorized the literature of the book of Jeremiah into three types and sources: poetic prophecies (A), biographical narratives (B), and prosaic sermons (C); C is generally seen as coming from Deuteronomistic hand (see Holladay, "Fresh Look" 394-95; Bright, "Date of the Prose" 15).

[13] Lundbom (806-07), following the LXX, believes that not the fathers but the current generation is the subject of the verse. He believes that there is haplography in the MT. I believe the MT reading is to be preferred.

[14] The bearing of the burden here is most likely connected with trade.

[15] E.g., H. Williamson, *Ezra and Nehemiah*, OTG 27; Clines, *Ezra* 205, 245. In fact, the whole of chapter 13 is believed to precede the whole of chapter 10 (e.g., H. Williamson, *Ezra-Nehemiah*, WBC 330-31; Clines, *Ezra* 199 and "Nehemiah 10" 112, 114).

[16] In addition, the household animals were to be allowed rest too (Exod. 20:10, 23:12; Deut. 5:14; cf. Exod. 34:21) but the Judahites were breaking the Sabbath also by making them work (Neh. 13:15).

[17] E.g., KJV, NIV, ESV, NASB, NRSV, NKJV, NLT, NET, NJB; cf. *BDB* (872, "assembly called at stated times for worship"); *BDB* 896; Lamberty-Zielinski (132, "sacred (cultic) assembly"); cf. Haag 394.

[18] On the contrary, Lamberty-Zielinski (133), contrasting מִקְרָא with קָהָל and עֵדָה, considers the former to refer to "an exclusive cultic assembly" (cf. *TWOT* 811).

[19] The same is achieved even by taking קֹדֶשׁ adjectivally but by avoiding 'assembly/convocation' for מִקְרָא; e.g., "sacred occasion."

[20] Levine contends that the *on* ending converts a noun into an adjective (*Leviticus* 210 n. 9).

[21] Adopted from Milgrom, *Leviticus 23-27*, 1952 where he gives a proposed chiastic structure of vv. 2b-4. My translation.

[22] See Mays 42; Laetsch 30; Waterman 185; cf. McCann 249; Haag 391; McKay, *Sabbath and Synagogue* 31-33.

[23] The nouns are translated in the plural taking them as collective singulars.

[24] Andersen and Freedman believe כָּל־מָשׂוֹשָׂהּ and וְכֹל מוֹעֲדָהּ form a "discontinuous hendiadys" referring to all of Israel's joyous occasions (250).

[25] Cf. Wood 177 ("set times"); Milgrom, *Leviticus 23-27*, 1932 ("fixed times"); Macintosh 61-62 ("festive occasions").

[26] Again the nouns are translated in the plural taking them as collective singulars.

[27] Morgenstern (316) takes קְרָא מִקְרָא to be a late interpolation. Our focus being on the final form, we consider the phrase very much a part of the text.

[28] Whybray states: ". . . but the thesis that nothing after chapter 39 can be attributed to the eighth-century prophet, and that chapters 40-66 cannot be pre-exilic has been almost universally accepted and remains the standard opinion up to the present time" (*Second Isaiah* 2).

[29] The universal outlook of the passage is clear from the immediate context as well: consider כָּל־הַגּוֹיִם וְהַלְּשֹׁנוֹת "all (the) nations and (the) tongues" (v. 18) and גּוֹיִם (vv. 19, 20). The structure of vv. 18-24 proposed by Motyer (540) also reflects the universal nature of this text:

A¹ A world-wide community envisaged (18-19)

    B A community of brothers accepted in Jerusalem (20-22)

A² A world-wide worshipping community in constant session (23-24)

[30] Hailey sees Isaianic "new heavens and the new earth" fulfilled in the coming of Christ, whereas "the new heavens and the new earth" of the NT (e.g., 2 Pet. 3:13) is to be fulfilled in His second advent (518-19, 528-29, 538-39).

[31] For a succinct coverage on the millennial view of the land of Israel, Davidic monarchy, temple and its cult, see Walvoord 147-52.

[32] Also note that, although some question it, the noun שַׁבָּת is related to the verb שָׁבַת at least in the OT (see Stolz 1297).

Chapter 3

Sabbatical Year and the Year of Jubilee

Sabbatical and Jubilee years are extensions of the Sabbath. As mentioned earlier, the study of these years will be brief because our focus is on the weekly Sabbath. A major concern of both these years is the rest (Sabbath) of/for the land by letting it lie fallow. Careful study of the regulations for these years reveals that besides rest for the land, they are given primarily for the benefit of the poor and the marginalized. These regulations prevent the poor and the vulnerable from being endlessly exploited by the rich and powerful. The regulations include release of slaves after six years of service, release of debts on the sabbatical year, release of debt-slaves and return of the land to the original owner in the Jubilee. Moreover, the beneficiaries of the natural produce of the fallow year include the poor and even the animals. Sabbatical year will be covered first and then the Jubilee. However, occasional intermingling cannot be avoided.

Exodus 23:10-11

This passage is the first appearance of the sabbatical year legislation in the Bible. Casperson sees the possibility of the passage belonging to the Mosaic era (283; cf. C. Wright, "What Happened, Part I" 130). The command is to let the land lie fallow on the seventh year. Stackert, however, believes that Exod. 23:10-11 does not require the land to be left fallow; rather it is to be sowed and harvested and the produce given to the poor. There is no sabbatical year in these verses (Stackert 244). This view is problematic. Firstly, the phrase comprised of two synonymous verbs תִּשְׁמְטֶנָּה וּנְטַשְׁתָּהּ ('let it lie fallow and untilled') clearly shows that the land is to be left fallow. Stackert provides no explanation for the phrase. Secondly, the vav that begins v. 11 (וְהַשְּׁבִיעָת) is certainly contrastive (cf. Table 2), which means v. 11a anticipates something that is opposite to the prescription in v. 10. Both of these show that the land was to be left fallow.

The purpose of letting the land lie fallow is (v. 11b): וְאָכְלוּ אֶבְיֹנֵי עַמֶּךָ וְיִתְרָם תֹּאכַל חַיַּת הַשָּׂדֶה ('so that the poor of your people may eat and the remainder the animals of the field may eat'). The vav in וְאָכְלוּ introduces the purpose clause. The poor of the land will have food and what they leave will be for wild animals (חַיַּת הַשָּׂדֶה is most probably a reference to the wild animals). The poor here are especially the landless (Noth, *Exodus* 190). The clear purpose then is purely humanitarian, which includes even the wild animals. In addition, the halt in sowing and reaping for a year also meant a lengthy period of near-rest for farmers and slaves in an agrarian society. Of course, other works needed to be done, but in an agrarian context, sowing and reaping is the principal activity. Hartley rightly comments on the sabbatical year, "God wants his people to be free from continuous labor in order that they might enjoy the gift of the promised land and the grace of his blessing" (433).

However, some believe that a farmer chose the rotation of the fallow year among his fields, vineyards, and orchards (Gerstenberger 375; see also Stuart, *Exodus* 531). If this is correct, then the agricultural work did not stop in any year for any household, which means there was no break from agricultural work and there was somewhat uniform production for a household year after year. This situation seems probable when one looks at Exod. 23:10-11 alone but when he/she considers Lev. 25, it becomes improbable. Lev. 25:20-22 speaks to a situation in which at least a household—not necessarily the whole nation—will have no sowing and reaping whatsoever in the sabbatical year.

Although one cannot be certain from this passage whether the fallow year was one fixed year for all the Israelites or it was practiced individually (see R. A. Cole 178), in all likelihood the latter was the case. That is, the fallow year differed from individual to individual. If the fallow year was the same nationwide, then the beneficiaries (v. 11b) would hardly find their sustenance; however, if it was individual, there would be some land fallow every year in every area, and this would make the sustenance of the poor possible (so also C. Wright, "What Happened, Part I" 130-31; Stuart, *Exodus* 531-32). In either case, it is certain that the legislation is very humanitarian (cf. the structure below). Childs notes: "In Exodus the social motivation comes to the fore" (*Exodus* 482).

Verses 10-11 have the same syntactical structure as v. 12 (see Table 2). Why was the land to be left fallow, and vineyards, orchards, and groves untended every seventh year? So that the poor primarily—and then the wild animals—may find sustenance.

Table 2: Structural comparison of Exod. 23:10-11 and Exod. 23:12

A	Positive	you shall	sow and gather *six* years (10)	work *six* days (12a)
B	Contrastive	but	let the land lie fallow (rest) the *seventh* (year) (11a)	cease (rest) the *seventh* day (12b)
C	Purpose	so that	the poor and the wild animals may eat (11b)	the cattle, slaves, and sojourners may rest and be refreshed (12c)
D	Addenda	do the same	with vineyard and olive garden (cf. A+B) (11c)	—

Moreover, vv. 10-11 is probably chiastic:

A sow and reap; forego (10-11a)

  B so that the poor and the wild animals may eat (11b)

A' do the same = tend and gather; forego (11c)

The purpose clause (B) applies to both injunctions (A and A'). The structure also shows that the primary concern of the sabbatical year in this text is the welfare of the poor; what they left was for the wild animals. In other words, the command is humanitarian.

Leviticus 25:1-7, 20-22

C. Wright holds that the sabbatical year has become one fixed year throughout the land in Lev. 25:1-7, unlike Exod. 23:10-11 (also Milgrom, *Leviticus 23-27*, 2155-56). He bases his argument on the supposed change of אַרְצֶךָ (Exod. 23:10) to הָאָרֶץ (Lev.

25:2, 4, 5, 6) (C. Wright, "What Happened, Part I" 131, 132).
However, as C. Wright also acknowledges, Lev. 25:1-7 too
uses second person singular injunctions (ibid.). The change
from אַרְצְךָ to הָאָרֶץ does not provide sufficient grounds to
conclude that the sabbatical year is the same year nationwide in
Lev. 25. The sabbatical year was probably individual as Stuart
also comments that neither Exod. 23 nor Lev. 25 requires it
to be the same year nationwide (*Exodus* 531).

The structure of vv. 1-7 should be looked at in the context
of the whole chapter. However, this little passage has the
following symmetrical structure:

Prologue (1-2a)

A   Sabbath for the land (2b)

  A' Sow and reap six years (3)

B   Sabbath for the land (4a)

  B' Do not sow or reap in this year (4b-5a)

C   Sabbath for the land (5b)

  C' What grows on its own in this year may be eaten (6-7)

Three times in this short text, the seventh year is said to be
a Sabbath for the land. Also interesting literarily is that the
root שׁבת appears seven times in the text, in keeping with the
sabbatical nature of the text: twice in v. 2, thrice in v. 4, once
each in vv. 5 and 6. Moreover, the list of beneficiaries of the
sabbatical year's natural produce includes seven categories. The
nature of the sabbatical year is also clarified by the superlative
שַׁבַּת שַׁבָּתוֹן ('Sabbath of complete rest') in v. 4. Interestingly,
v. 2b says that *the land shall observe the Sabbath* to/for YHWH.
The land is personified. Of course, humans are in control of
whether the land can keep the Sabbath or not, which is clear

from the explication. Each time the Sabbath of the land is mentioned (A, B, C), some injunction follows clarifying what the humans were to do (or not do) (A', B', C').[1] The Sabbath observance by the land is so important that if its inhabitants do not allow this to happen, YHWH will enforce the Sabbath upon the land (Lev. 26:34-35, 42-43).

וְהָיְתָה שַׁבַּת הָאָרֶץ לָכֶם לְאָכְלָה (v. 6) is obscure. 'And the Sabbath of the land shall be for you for food' is perhaps the best literal translation. The idea most probably is that the Sabbath year's natural produce shall be food for those listed following the phrase. תִּהְיֶה כָל־תְּבוּאָתָהּ לֶאֱכֹל ('all its produce shall be for food,' v. 7) that ends the pericope suggests that such is the case. The list of beneficiaries is sandwiched between these two phrases. However, this provision seems to contradict v. 5 which says that what grows naturally should not be harvested or gathered. Some believe the inference here is that the aftergrowth is for consumption alone by the beneficiaries listed and not to be harvested for storage and/or sale like in the non-sabbatical years (Milgrom, *Leviticus 23-27*, 2160, 2162; Hartley 434). In fact, Milgrom holds that the dual use of אכל in vv. 6-7 is emphatic (*Leviticus 23-27*, 2160, 2162). Gerstenberger, on the other hand, thinks that harvesting the aftergrowth of the cultivated land (שָׂדֶה, v. 4) was prohibited but of uncultivated or open land (אֶרֶץ) was not (375-76). Precise understanding of the injunctions seems impossible today. However, what is certain is that there would be enough provision (cf. vv. 20-22).

Lev. 25:1-7 expands the concept found in Exod. 23:10-11 (so also Noth, *Leviticus* 185-86). Nothing new is added as such save an explanation for the regulation in Exod. 23:10-11. However, two things are of interest. First, the Sabbath of the land is said to be to/for YHWH (vv. 2, 4). Based on the use of שַׁבָּת לַיהוָה and שַׁבַּת שַׁבָּתוֹן, C. Wright says that the religious aspect of the law is emphasized in Lev. 25 ("What Happened, Part I" 131). Although religious connotation cannot be denied because the Israelites knew no law that was non-religious, there is nothing typically religious about שַׁבַּת שַׁבָּתוֹן, which means 'Sabbath of complete rest' (see chapter 2). Also, שַׁבָּת לַיהוָה (v. 2; cf. Exod. 20:10; Lev. 23:3; Deut. 5:14) simply says that the Sabbath is observed to/for YHWH without any further elucidation; no particular religious *activity* is prescribed. The phrase likely means simply that observing the Sabbath honors YHWH (see Hartley 433). Moreover, *the land*, rather than the humans, is expected to observe the Sabbath. In other words, the religious dimension is not any clearer in Lev. 25:1-7 than it is in Exod. 23:10-11. The humanitarian dimension, on the other hand, is clear.

Second, the list of beneficiaries of the sabbatical year's natural produce in Lev. 25:6-7 does not mention the poor. This omission is probably the reason C. Wright finds the humanitarian concern of Exod. 23:10-11 removed in Lev. 25:1-7 (see "What Happened, Part I" 131-32). The beneficiaries are the owner and those in relation to him (vv. 6-7) who would have been his responsibility anyway. However, there is an exception, namely, wild animals (וְלַחַיָּה אֲשֶׁר בְּאַרְצֶךָ). The exclusion of the poor from the list is puzzling. Nonetheless, if the Leviticus account depends on and expands the Exodus account as C. Wright too believes ("What Happened, Part I" 131-32), then it is safe to infer that the former does not exclude the poor but presupposes them.[2] Regarding the absence of the land-fallow regulation in Deut. 15 (more below), C. Wright believes that the text "has taken for granted the existence of the fallow year" because it depends on Exod. 23:10-11 and Lev. 25:1-7 ("What Happened,

Part I" 133-34). The same principle applies to the dependence of Lev. 25:1-7 on Exod. 23:10-11; the former presupposes the poor as beneficiaries and extends it to include those of the owner's household. If this is correct, then Lev. 25:1-7 is no less humanitarian.[3]

The command to the Israelites for the sabbatical year is to not sow and reap on the seventh year but to let the land rest or observe Sabbath. The obvious and probably instant question of the people to such a command would be, 'Then what shall we eat in the seventh year (and the eighth?)? The text anticipates the concern and addresses it but the readers have to wait for a while. The issue is addressed in vv. 20-22. Literarily, here again we encounter the utilization of suspense. People's anxiety is addressed after a digression. The anticipated question is spelled out in v. 20 and the answer to it comes in vv. 21-22. YHWH says that if the Israelites trust Him to allow the land a Sabbath on the seventh year, He will so bless the harvest of the sixth year that the land will produce triple and they will be eating the produce of the sixth year until the ninth year when the post-Sabbath crop will be harvested. Sabbath for the land is so important that the exile is perceived as its enforced Sabbath because of the Israelites' denial to voluntarily allow that Sabbath (Lev. 26:34-35, 43; 2 Chron. 36:21).

Deuteronomy 15:1-11[4]

This passage extends the sabbatical year law of fallow land to remission of debts (so also C. Wright, "What Happened, Part I" 132, 133). The phrase מִקֵּץ שֶׁבַע־שָׁנִים (v. 1) probably means in the (every) seventh year (Driver 174). However, in an agrarian context, loans were normally taken in the spring for sowing and paid off at the end of the year after harvesting;

thus, מִקֵּץ is possibly referring to the release of debts *at the end* of the seventh year (C. Wright, "What Happened, Part I" 132-33; Pruitt 86).

What was to be released is not clear. The syntax of שָׁמוֹט כָּל־בַּעַל מַשֵּׁה יָדוֹ אֲשֶׁר יַשֶּׁה בְּרֵעֵהוּ (v. 2) is difficult. The following are the major suggestions (see C. Wright, "What Happened, Part I" 134-38; McConville 255). First, כָּל־בַּעַל מַשֵּׁה יָדוֹ is taken as the subject and אֲשֶׁר יַשֶּׁה בְּרֵעֵהוּ as the object of the verb שָׁמוֹט. So, the implication is that every creditor should cancel the loan owed to him. Second, with the same syntax, מַשֵּׁה is understood to be the pledge taken as security on the loan, which means the loan is not remitted but the pledge is to be given back (see North 196-99). Third, כָּל־בַּעַל alone is considered the subject meaning 'every creditor' and מַשֵּׁה (hiphil participle) as the object, a verbal noun. Thus, 'every creditor shall release him who has taken loan by his hand (or handshake) which he has loaned to his friend.' This interpretation would mean that the person or the debtor is the one to be released. The implication is that the debtor has become a debt-slave to the creditor. The first option seems to make the best sense.

Similarly, the phrase וַאֲשֶׁר יִהְיֶה לְךָ אֶת־אָחִיךָ תַּשְׁמֵט יָדֶךָ (v. 3) is obscure, too. Syntactically, there are three main possibilities (see McConville 256). These provide the same three options as does v. 2. First, אָחִיךָ is considered the direct object with אֶת as its marker. Thus, the debtor—'your brother'—is to be released. Second, אֲשֶׁר יִהְיֶה לְךָ אֶת־אָחִיךָ is considered the direct object and אֶת as preposition (e.g., NASB). Thus, what is yours that is with your brother—the loan—is to be released. Third, the same syntax is preferred in which אֶת means 'in respect of.' This option does not clarify much; that thing with respect to your brother is to be released, which could be loan or pledge. The plain meaning of the phrase seems to be that the debt itself needs remission, i.e., the second interpretation is preferable. However, we cannot be dogmatic about it. Those who believe that the pledge rather than the debt was to be released differ on what the pledge would have been: the debtor himself, someone subject to the debtor (e.g., child or slave), or land (see C. Wright, "What Happened, Part I" 136).

Moreover, the manner of release is also a matter of debate. Was whatever was released temporary or permanent? Many believe the former is the case. Some among these believe that the repayment of debt was *suspended* for the period of the sabbatical year but not completely cancelled primarily because this would discourage any loan giving; moreover, the suspension was granted because the repayment in the sabbatical year would be impossible as a result of leaving the land fallow (e.g., Pruitt 86, 92; Craigie 236). Along the same line, C. Wright believes that the land pledged to the creditor and now in the creditor's usufruct was to be released for the sabbatical year for the debtor's use. This release of usufruct would provide some relief to the debtor through its production, although not much because it is a fallow year. On the other hand, it would not be a big sacrifice for the creditor (C. Wright, "What Happened, Part I" 137).

Often these discussions are influenced by the modern mindset. YHWH demanded extraordinary measures from the Israelites because they were His people whom He had delivered from extreme oppression in Egypt. Thus, He required them to treat each other with dignity. The permanent release of complete debt against one's poor neighbor would not be an impossible demand (cf. Miller, *Deuteronomy* 135). Cairns concurs that "the language of the text gives the firm impression that the Deuteronomists envisaged total cancellation of the debt" (147). The warning of 15:7-11 makes the best sense if the debt was to be completely cancelled. If only the pledge was to be released and/or if the release of debt/pledge was only deferred, then the warning is hardly necessary. In addition, the promised blessing in v. 10 also provides motivation to release the debts completely and permanently. In any case, the law sought to provide some sort of relief to the Israelites who were drowning in debt. As such, the law is undoubtedly humanitarian despite the ambiguity of the details of its implementation.

Deut. 31:9-13 assumes a fixed sabbatical year in Israel and requires the law (probably Deuteronomy) to be read to the people assembled during Succoth (the festival of booths) in that year. Communal worship is certainly involved here. However, this is secondary; it happens when people gather to celebrate Succoth. The primary concerns are rest for the land and release of debts.

Moreover, the extension of the sabbatical year is found in the law of letting the slaves go free in the seventh year, i.e., after six years of service, to which we now turn. The concern is purely humanitarian.

Exodus 21:2-11

Verses 2-6 deal with a male slave bought by an Israelite. He was to be released after six years of service without having to pay for his freedom (v. 2). Three situations are posited (vv. 3-4). First, if the slave was acquired single and remained single until the time of release, he went away alone. Second, if he came in married, he was released along with his wife (presumably their children, if any, were released too). Third, if the master provided the slave with a wife during his servitude, he left alone; the wife and children remained the master's property. However, the slave could choose to forego his freedom and serve his master for life, and this was achieved through an ear piercing rite (vv. 5-6).

Noth believes that vv. 7-11 talk about female slavery in which a girl is sold by her father either to be a slave or a wife; her rights will be determined based on whether she is only a slave, and thus a 'thing,' or a wife in which case she will have some rights. The distinction that a male slave may be released (vv. 2-6) but a female slave may not is possibly based on the thought that man is a 'person' while woman is a 'possession'; later Deut. 15:12-18 does away with this distinction (Noth, *Exodus* 177-79). Enns believes she is sold either to be the master's slave or his son's wife; he does not see her being the master's wife (444). Both Noth and Enns see here the either/or, i.e., slave or wife. However, Van Seters is correct that the verses deal with a daughter sold in marriage as a 'slave-wife' for the purchaser or his son; it does not apply to all female slaves ("Law" 1996: 542-43; 2007: 173-76; cf. W. Kaiser, "Exodus" 430). Some fail to adequately consider this fact and take the verses to be applicable to female slaves in general (e.g., Brueggemann, "Exodus" 862; Noth, *Exodus* 177-79; Enns 444). She is not to be released like the male slave except in case of the violation of her marital rights because she is not a typical slave but also a wife. The text is silent about the female slaves that are not wives. For that we have to look at Deut. 15:12-18, to which we now turn.

Deuteronomy 15:12-18

This passage has the same guidelines concerning both male and female slaves. The owner should release them after six years of service (v. 12) and provide sufficient provisions while releasing (vv. 13-14). The context suggests that the injunction for provisions is also applicable to both male and female slaves (vv. 12, 17b) (cf. Van Seters, "Law" 2007: 175-76). The provisions were probably meant for starting life afresh (so Clements 66; Nelson 197; Merrill 245-46). The provisions merely involve sharing some from the bountiful blessings that YHWH has bestowed upon the master (v. 14). The slave owners are to remember that they too were slaves in Egypt and YHWH redeemed them; they should thus keep the commandment (v. 15). However, the slave may choose to serve the master for life (vv. 16-17). The word מִשְׁנֶה in v. 18 is perhaps a technical term meaning 'equivalent to' (Tsevat 125-26; see also Thompson, *Deuteronomy* 191; NRSV), not 'double' (NASB) or 'half' (ESV). In any case, the master should not be reluctant in letting the slave go free, and YHWH will bless him for it (v. 18).

Leviticus 25:8-55

This passage deals with the year of Jubilee. The concern is the varied negative situations in which a person can find himself due to debt and the ways to reverse them. The following simplified structure of the passage gives a picture.[5]

Jubilee proclamation and basic stipulations (8-12)

Situations brought about by debt (13-55)

    Case 1: Selling land (13-28)

        Sabbatical year (20-22)

Case 2: Selling house (29-34)

Case 3: An Israelite becomes internal immigrant (35-38)

Case 4: An Israelite sells himself or becomes enslaved (39-55)

   Case 4a: An Israelite sells himself to another Israelite (39-46)

      An Israelite's foreigner-slave (44-46a)

   Case 4b: An Israelite sells himself to a foreigner (47-55)

There is a clear structure here, a downward spiral, in which the situation occurring from debt is arranged in the ascending order of severity (cf. Chirichigno, 323f; Schenker 37, 40). First, the land, most probably a portion, is sold and then the house; after losing both, one could be forced to migrate (internally) resulting in heavy borrowing. In a more serious situation, he might sell himself to another Israelite, and in the worst case, he might sell himself to a foreigner in his own land. The case of a foreigner becoming a slave to an Israelite (vv. 44-46a) is distinct but it is dealt with in the context of an Israelite having to sell himself in order to admonish that an Israelite master is not to behave with another Israelite like with a foreign slave. The bracketing (inclusio) of the material on foreign slaves with the injunction against ruling a fellow Israelite (slave) with harshness (vv. 43 and 46b) shows that the text's real concern is the Israelite and not the foreigner. In contrasting the two, however, we learn how the foreign slave could be treated. The key word in relation to the Jubilee is "return" (שׁוּב) and the key verse is v. 10 (so also Shead 21). The Israelites were allowed to return to their own land and clan (מִשְׁפָּחָה).

Verses 8-12 give the basic principles/instructions. The beginning of the Jubilee was marked by the trumpet sound on the Day of Atonement. The year is holy and the land is to be left fallow as done in the sabbatical year. Proclamation of freedom/liberty (דְּרוֹר), and return to one's property and clan are central.

There are some obscurities regarding the Jubilee. Did it occur every 49 years (e.g., Bergsma 121-25) or every 50 years (e.g., Kawashima 117-20), or did it stretch from the 49th to the 50th year beginning on the tenth day of the seventh month of the 49th year (see Lemche, "Manumission" 46-47)?[6] Was the Jubilee and the seventh sabbatical year identical (e.g., Y. Kim 147-49; Chirichigno 317-21) or did Jubilee follow the latter (e.g., Rooker, *Leviticus* 304)? Was the Jubilee a short year of 49 days (e.g., Hoenig 222-36; Wenham, *Leviticus* 319)? We need not dwell in the details here because our interest lies in the concerns of the Jubilee which are unaffected by the answers to these questions. Let us look one by one at each case brought about by debt.

The first case (vv. 13-28) entails selling one's land. The land is not sold in the real sense because it has to come back to the original owner; so it is more akin to leasing. However, the word used here is מָכַר. What is sold in fact is the crop and so the cost of the land should be based on the number of years to the approaching Jubilee (vv. 14-17). If a person is forced to sell his land, his kin or he himself has the right to redeem it (vv. 25-27). In case no redemption occurs, the land is to be returned to the original owner in the Jubilee (v. 28). Verses 20-22 deal with the sabbatical year and look like a digression but they too deal with land and crops. Moreover, the promise of a bumper crop in the sixth year making it possible for the land to be left fallow in the sabbatical year applies for the Jubilee as well.

The second case (vv. 29-34) deals with the sale of a house. If a house in a walled city is sold, then it may be redeemed within a year of its sale, but if not redeemed within the year, the house will belong to the purchaser; it need not be released in the Jubilee (vv. 29-30). A house in an unwalled village is to be treated like land and hence may be redeemed any time; if not redeemed, it must be released in the Jubilee (v. 31). As for the Levites' houses in the cities, they may be redeemed any time and released in the Jubilee if not redeemed earlier (vv. 32-33), and their pasturelands may not be sold (v. 34). The likely reason for this exception is that the Levites did not own agricultural land in the villages (cf. Harris 636; Hartley 439-40).

The third case (vv. 35-38) concerns a situation in which an Israelite becomes internal immigrant as Schenker (29-31) has argued although the passage is usually understood as an injunction to not charge interest and usury to an impoverished neighbor. The injunction, however, is that if any Israelite becomes impoverished and is forced to migrate, he should be allowed to live like a sojourner (גֵּר or תּוֹשָׁב) within the land of Israel. The Israelites of the place that he migrates to should welcome him in their midst. The migration most probably would be along with the household. Moreover, the migration would cause the person to borrow further. Schenker is correct that vv. 36-37 should be understood in this context, i.e., the Israelites there should not charge interest and take advantage of the migrant countryman and his family. The verses do not ban all forms of interest or usury (Schenker 29-30). In dealing with these immigrants, the Israelites are to remember that they too were immigrants in Egypt and YHWH brought

them out from there to give the land in which they now live
(v. 38). These were probably temporary internal immigrants
who would be able to return to their property and clan in the
Jubilee. They probably lost their property to debt and were
forced to migrate.

The fourth case (vv. 39-55) involves an Israelite paterfamilias
forced to sell himself for the service of another (Chirichigno
330; cf. Schenker 32, 33).[7] The clear words of the text deny that
an Israelite can be a slave to another person because they are
YHWH's slaves (vv. 39-40a, 42, 55). However, the conditions
are not quite different from that of a slave except that the
masters are admonished not to deal with them harshly.

There are two situations of a paterfamilias' servitude.
First (vv. 39-46), he sells himself—along with his family—to
another Israelite. They shall not be treated like slaves but like
hired laborers, and they shall be released in the Jubilee to
go back to their clan and property. Second (vv. 47-55), the
paterfamilias sells himself to a foreigner in the former's own
land. This is the worst situation envisioned. In this situation,
the one enslaved or his kin has the right of redemption (vv.
48-49). The redemption price will depend upon the original
sale price, the number of years served, and the approaching
Jubilee (vv. 50-52). The enslaved should be treated as a hired
laborer and not dealt with harshly while in servitude (v. 53).
If no redemption occurs, then he must be released with his
family in the Jubilee (v. 54). The reason is that the Israelites
are YHWH's slaves (v. 55).

In both the cases involving paterfamilias, release comes
in the Jubilee along with his household (vv. 41, 54). However,
unlike v. 41, v. 54 only mentions release of the slave and his

family but return to one's property is not mentioned. The likely reason is that the foreign master could not lay any claim on an Israelite's patrimonial land even momentarily (Gerstenberger 392).

Verses 44-46a deal with an Israelite's foreign slave. As argued earlier, this section is given to contrast a foreign slave from a native who has sold himself in order to communicate that the Israelite master may not deal with fellow Israelite like he does with a foreign slave. And yes, foreign slaves can be treated like slaves and they may even be passed on as property to the future generation; there is no need to release them.

Exodus 21:2-11; Deuteronomy 15:12-18; and Leviticus 25:39-43

An important issue concerning the manumission of slaves is the relation between these three texts. Most believe that the texts are interrelated. Some say that Leviticus revises the provision of six year service in Exod. 21 and Deut. 15, and extends the period which may be up to fifty years; however, balance is sought by admonishing the slave owners to deal with their subjects like hired laborers (not slaves) and without harshness (e.g., De Vaux 83). Some try to harmonize by saying that the slave release took place after six years of service unless the Jubilee year came before the completion of six years (e.g., Sarna 119; R. Harrison, *Leviticus* 227). Similarly, some believe that Lev. 25 provides "exception" to Exod. 21 and Deut. 15 in that the slave who committed himself to serve the master for life was also to be released in the Jubilee together with his wife and children even though he had acquired them while in the master's service (Hartley 433; cf. Rooker, *Leviticus* 303; W. Kaiser, "Leviticus" 1172).

C. Wright, however, argues that while Exod. 21 and Deut. 15 deal with identical situations, Lev. 25 deals with a different one. He makes this distinction based on, among other things, the word "Hebrew" which is found in the first two texts but not in Lev. 25. The term "Hebrew" is not ethnic but refers to a social class that was landless who made their living by serving in others' houses; "Hebrew" is not identical to "Israelite."[8] On the contrary, Lev. 25 deals with the Israelites who owned land but had been subjected to service of another due to debts. They could thus return to their property and clan once released in the Jubilee. The release of Exod. 21 and Deut. 15 took place individually after six years of service but that of Lev. 25 occurred nationwide in the Jubilee (C. Wright, "What Happened, Part II" 195-99). Wright rightly understands the distinct case in Lev. 25. However, I believe that even Exod. 21 and Deut. 15 deal with different situations. The following are the reasons for this suggestion (cf. McConville 262-63).

First, as Van Seters contends, unlike Deut. 15:12-18 that deals with a free person sold due to debt, Exod. 21:2-6 deals with a person who probably was already a slave (עֶבֶד עִבְרִי) of another—a foreigner—at the time of his purchase (קָנָה) by an Israelite ("Law," 1996: 536, 540; 2007: 171-72; cf. Clements 27). This view is strengthened by the fact that in Deut. 15, as McConville (262) has noted, the person in servitude is not called slave prior to his choice to be so for life in v. 17.

Second, while the "Hebrew" man/woman is called "your brother/sister" (אָחִיךָ) in Deut. 15:12, such is not the case in Exod. 21. Thus, the "Hebrew" of Exod. 21 is probably a foreign slave but of Deut. 15 is an ethnic Israelite (see Von Rad 107; Nelson 197).

Third, the injunction for generous provisions at the time of release in Deut. 15:13-14 is not just an addition to or extension of Exod. 21:2-6. The provisions were probably for a fresh start. The person released was probably not landless either. In fact, McConville contends that the text does not conclude that the released slave was landless; rather it assumes that he/she owns property to which he/she can return (263). On the other hand, no provisions are prescribed in Exod. 21 possibly because the person was, as argued, already a slave prior to this owner and was landless. As such he would probably continue his slavery elsewhere even if he chose release in the seventh year. The release was prescribed likely to protect him from the possible lifelong slavery under a harsh master. He, however, was free to choose lifelong service with the master; this would happen either because of his love for the master or for his family acquired while in servitude or both (v. 5). The choice of lifelong service may also occur because he perceives that his life is better off with the current master than he would possibly find elsewhere.

Lev. 25:39-43, on the other hand, deals with the indentured Israelite head of the family. Tigay comments that the one who sold himself to servitude (together with his family) may even die before the Jubilee and never be freed but his family will eventually be free. Similarly, the return of the land in the Jubilee may occur only after the debtor's death but his children will eventually regain it. In this schema, then, family and clan are more important (Tigay 467).

Let us sum up this discussion. Exod. 21:2-6 probably deals with a landless non-Israelite who was already a slave and is now bought by another. No provisions are required at the time of his release in the seventh year because he does not have means (e.g., land) to start life as a free or independent person. He will likely be a slave of another master if he chooses release. He has the choice to continue serving his current master for life. This case is not one of debt-slavery.

Deut. 15:12-18 probably deals with an Israelite man or woman sold (or self-sold) to temporary servitude due to debts. He/she is to be released after six years and given generous provisions to enable a fresh start. He/she likely owns property to which they can return. Lifelong service to the master can be opted. This text places male and female debt-slaves on equal footing. The case of the female slave in Exod. 21:7-11 is different (cf. Tigay 148-49). There a father sells his daughter as a slave-wife for the purchaser or his son. The text does not apply to female slaves that are not slave-wives.

Lev. 25:39-43 deals with an Israelite paterfamilias who sells himself along with his family to servitude. He owns land that he will regain in the Jubilee when he will be released from indenture and can start afresh again.

There are two rationales for jubilee legislation as Shead (22) has noted: (1) the Israelites cannot own the land because it belongs to YHWH (Lev. 25:23), and (2) the Israelites are YHWH's slaves, so they cannot be another's slave (Lev. 25:42, 55). The first prohibited the Israelites from selling their land perpetually and the second prohibited them from enslaving a fellow-Israelite. The essence of the Jubilee can be summed up in Hubbard's words: "Since [YHWH] owns Canaan, his policy is that families retain, not lose, their inherited land. Since he owns Israel, his policy is that his people never see perpetual slavery again" (12). Thus, YHWH functions as a גאל each Jubilee; this echoes in some small way the exodus from Egypt (Hartley 442; Hubbard 11-12).

The practical observances of the Jubilee year (or its kind) are found in Jer. 34:8f and Neh. 5:1-13. These seem to be occasional observances by the order or initiative of a king (Zedekiah) and a governor (Nehemiah), not the Jubilee year itself. Nonetheless, the principles of sabbatical and Jubilee years are in operation. Similarly, Neh. 10:31b[32b] records the vow to observe the sabbatical year in the postexilic period.

Summary

Although the relative brevity of this chapter cannot do proper justice to this vast subject and the substantial biblical text covered, we have dealt with the most fundamental issues. Several insights emerge. Fundamental to both the sabbatical and Jubilee years is the rest/Sabbath for the land, i.e., letting the land lie fallow. In fact, it is so important that the exile is seen as the forced Sabbath for the land because of the failure of the Israelites to allow it. Most probably the land lying fallow was to be observed individually by the farmers and was not a fixed year nationwide. The beneficiaries of the natural produce of the fallow year included the poor and the wild animals. However, Deuteronomy (15:1-11, 31:9-13) envisages a nationwide sabbatical year in which the debts are released, and the law is read during the festival of tabernacles. The sabbatical year principle is also seen in the command to release one's slaves after six years of their service. In addition to letting the land lie fallow, the Jubilee involved releasing the paterfamilias debt-slave and returning the land to the original owner. Hence, every Jubilee provided the opportunity for a fresh start to those Israelite heads of the family who had lost their patrimonial land and/or were reduced to debt-slavery.

Therefore, in addition to the rest for the land, the sabbatical and Jubilee years are concerned with the welfare of the poor and the vulnerable. Although the religious connotation of these years cannot be denied because Israel knew nothing that was non-religious, the law was purely humanitarian whose concern extends even to the land. Two things are crucial, viz., rest for the land and relief for the poor. The only explicit "worship" requirement is found in Deut. 31:9-13 that of reading the law in the assembly of those gathered to celebrate Succoth in the sabbatical year.

Endnotes

[1] While acknowledging this fact, U. Kim, however, entertains the thought that the earth is probably obligated and capable of observing the Sabbath without human cooperation (see 397).

[2] Contra Milgrom, *Leviticus 23-27*, 2154, 2160. Could it also be that the exclusion of the poor was because its inclusion would make the list of beneficiaries have eight entries? As noted earlier, in keeping with the sabbatical nature of the text, the list includes seven categories (cf. Exod. 20:10). To this, it could, however, be argued that any other item could have been excluded instead of "poor." However, the list also shows another characteristic which would be disturbed if "poor" was included at the expense of another. The list of beneficiaries comes in pairs except "you" (with seven one has to stand alone)—male and female slaves, hired and resident men, domestic and wild animals.

[3] Furthermore, neither C. Wright nor Milgrom explains the inclusion of wild animals.

[4] Nelson (194, 196) proposes chiastic structures of vv. 2-3 and of vv. 7-11.

[5] Many scholars perceive a long process of development in arriving to the current text. Although there is no consensus about the stages and the process, see, for a sample, Fager (123-25) who sees five "strata" in Lev. 25:8-55.

[6] Some, however, believe that the tenth day of the seventh month marked the New Year's Day (e.g., Noth, *Leviticus* 172f, 185, 186).

[7] While Schenker (31-32) prefers passive meaning ('to be sold') of the niphal of מָכַר (vv. 39, 47; Deut. 15:12), many others suggest that both passive and reflexive ('sell himself') meanings are possible (e.g., Chirichigno 329-32; Tigay 149; McConville 262). The reflexive interpretation means that a person sells himself into slavery. The passive interpretation could mean a dependent has been sold. In Lev. 25 reflexive seems more likely, whereas in Deut. 15 either is possible.

[8] Many believe that "Hebrew" was a non-ethnic term at least in earlier biblical times and referred to a lower social class, especially those who sold themselves into slavery (e.g., J. Lewy 1-13; Alt 93-96; Ellison 30-35; cf. Bright, *History of Israel* 93-95; McConville 256). At the heart of this argument is the proposed etymological association between עִבְרִי (Hebrew) and the Akkadian *ḫabiru*, *'abiru* or *'apiru*, although this connection has been questioned (e.g., Tigay 148; Hyatt 228). Nonetheless, some have reached the same conclusion based on the biblical texts as well (J. Lewy 1-8; Alt 94-95). J. Lewy contends that the identification of the Israelites (and Judahites) and their language as "Hebrew" is an intertestamental development (2), whereas Tigay believes "Hebrew" to be "the oldest designation for Israelites" used before Jacob was named Israel and until the time prior to David's reign (148). Moreover, while some believe that a "Hebrew" was a non-Israelite (e.g., J. Lewy 1-13), others believe he was an Israelite (e.g., Tigay 148), and yet others believe he could have been an Israelite or a foreigner (e.g., Lemche, "Hebrew Slave" 136-44). Von Rad, on the other hand, believes that the "Hebrew" of Exod. 21 is non-ethnic and refers to those of lower social class but of Deut. 15 is an ethnic Israelite (107; cf. Nelson 197). Likewise, some believe that חָפְשִׁי (Exod. 21:2; Deut. 15:12) denotes someone who is neither a slave nor a fully freedman, but somewhere between the two (e.g., Lemche, "Hebrew Slave" 139-42), while others believe that it denotes a completely free individual once released (e.g., Phillips, "Laws of Slavery" 59; McConville 262).

Chapter 4

Sabbath, New Testament, and the Church Today

If we are to make sense of the Sabbath for our times, then the NT witness to it is essential. The Christ event is crucial in understanding the OT law including the Sabbath for today. Therefore, this chapter will first study a few NT texts that are believed to have direct bearing on the Sabbath law in the aftermath of the Christ event. These texts will be studied briefly because this work is primarily a study of the OT Sabbath. The chapter will then discuss how the Sabbath can be applied today in light of the NT witness.

Mark 2:27

Jesus, time and again, was involved in a controversy with the Jewish religious leaders regarding Sabbath observance, but Mark 2:27 records His most informative words on the subject. The verse reads:

> καὶ ἔλεγεν αὐτοῖς· τὸ σάββατον διὰ τὸν ἄνθρωπον ἐγένετο καὶ οὐχ ὁ ἄνθρωπος διὰ τὸ σάββατον·

> And [Jesus] said to them, "The Sabbath was made for the man and not the man for the Sabbath."

The verse is used in the context of Jesus' disciples plucking the heads of grain while walking through grain-fields on a Sabbath (Mark 2:23-28[1]). The Pharisees complained that the disciples were breaking the Sabbath; presumably the plucking was seen as harvesting. Jesus replied by drawing attention to the incident in 1 Sam. 21:1-6 when David and company violated the law when they ate of the showbread. The then high priest was also involved in breaking the law.[2] Then he spoke the words of v. 27 followed by his assertion that He is Lord even of the Sabbath (v. 28).[3] The parallel accounts in Mt. 12:1-8 and Luke 6:1-5 lack the words of v. 27 but only record Jesus' claim of lordship over the Sabbath. The point of David and company eating the forbidden bread and still being 'not guilty' probably has to do with the fact that human need is more important than legalistic or inflexible adherence to the law; David and his men were starving (so Brooks 66; L. Williamson 73).[4] This message is probably what Jesus is trying to communicate in Mark 2:23-28.

Some, however, take the passage to mean that since Jesus is the Lord of the Sabbath, He can permit breaking the Sabbath (e.g., Parsons 57-60). Parsons holds that vv. 27-28 comprise a rhetorical device called "enthymemic chreia"[5] and thus the message of the verses is: the Sabbath is made for man but since Jesus is no ordinary man but the Lord of the Sabbath, He has the authority to permit His disciples to break the Sabbath (59).[6] The proposal is interesting but Parsons does not deal adequately with the mention of the Davidic event. Although it is true that the text is primarily about the lordship of Christ over the Sabbath, particularly looking at the parallel accounts in

Matthew and Luke, the mention of the Davidic event suggests that there is more here than an affirmation of Jesus' lordship over the Sabbath. The message seems that human need takes precedence over stringent adherence to the law. In fact, Parsons admits to this fact (twice in p. 58). Moreover, Parsons' view that the text is alluding to the fulfillment of Isaianic prophecy (see Isa. 40:3) of 'preparing the way of the Lord' (58) seems to be an overstretch.

Many follow a slightly different line of thought that if David as a person in authority was not guilty when he broke the law, Jesus as the Son of David and the Messiah has greater authority, and hence can override the Sabbath commandment (e.g., France 145-48). Although the text is Christological and Messianic (see v. 28), this interpretation is doubtful. The simple conclusion allowed by the narrative is that human need takes precedence over strict law adherence, in this case, the Sabbath. Lohse rightly comments, "In Mk. 2:27, however, man and his needs are said to be of greater value than the commandment" ("σάββατον" 22). Presumably the disciples were hungry (cf. Mt. 12:1). That the Sabbath was a humanitarian law from the very beginning is very evident here.

Some sabbatarians interpret v. 27 to mean human beings are liable to keep the Sabbath because Jesus said that it was made for man. If it was made for humans, the argument goes, then it means that they are bound to observe it (e.g., Lee 195). While it is true that Jesus is not denying the observance of the Sabbath, it is not the purpose of the text to defend Sabbath observance either. Rather, as the immediate context makes it clear, the text is attempting to communicate that the Sabbath, and in fact the whole law, was made for the benefit of humans, not the other way round. In essence, Jesus was refuting the

Pharisaic notion of Sabbath observance which was ridiculously unbearable; and hence, instead of the Sabbath being a delight, which is what the command intended it to be, it had become a heavy burden. All in all, Jesus is redefining the significance of the Sabbath and restoring it to the original purpose which the religious leaders of His time had lost in their extreme legalism. Lohse is correct: "The absolute obligation of the commandment is thus challenged, though its validity is not contested in principle" ("σάββατον" 22).

Colossians 2:16

Col. 2:16 is the clearest reference to the Sabbath in the Pauline corpus.[7] The verse reads:

> Μὴ οὖν τις ὑμᾶς κρινέτω ἐν βρώσει καὶ ἐν πόσει ἢ ἐν μέρει ἑορτῆς ἢ νεομηνίας ἢ σαββάτων·

> Therefore, do not let anyone judge you concerning food and (concerning) drink, or concerning observance of a festival or a New Moon or Sabbaths.

The message seems straightforward: matters of food, drink, festivals, special days, etc. are trivial. No one should be judged based upon their diet and their observance or nonobservance of these religious occasions. Blomberg notes that "the vast majority of interpreters" take the 'food and drink' to refer to both the Jewish dietary law and to the eating-drinking associated with pagan festivals ("Sabbath as Fulfilled," *Perspectives* 344). Some, on the other hand, believe that the ascetic-type prohibition of food and drink is in view because the Jewish dietary law did not involve prohibition of drinks (e.g., Bruce, *Colossians* 113-14; O'Brien 138).[8] However, the broader OT food and drink laws are probably in view, which include regular dietary law and Nazirite-type prohibitions (see Barth and Blanke 338).[9]

The verse most likely does not include activities related to pagan festivals.

The combination festival-new moon-Sabbaths likely refers to the annual, monthly, and weekly Israelite celebrations (cf. Hos. 2:11[13]) (so also Barth and Blanke 339).[10] Not everyone concurs. Scholars have long been debating about the nature of the "Colossian heresy" that Paul is refuting in the epistle.[11] Some, however, have questioned the whole notion of a "Colossian heresy" (e.g., Hooker 121-36; see also Asher 107-22). Many, nonetheless, see some form of heresy being refuted in 2:16-17 as well (e.g., Murray 178). O'Brien contends especially in light of v. 20 that Paul is refuting here not the observance of festivals and days per se but those observances "bound up with the recognition of the elemental spirits"[12] (139). Whatever may be the broader context of the epistle, 2:16-17 most probably deals with Jewish calendric observances and OT food-drink laws rather than syncretistic or pagan ones (see Barth and Blanke 338; Dunn, *Colossians* 171-75; Pipa 146).[13] This fact is clear from v. 17 also. The regulations listed in v. 16 are considered the shadow (σκιά) of the substance (σῶμα), namely, Christ (or 'Christ's').[14] How can syncretistic or pagan religious practices be the "shadow" of Christ (cf. Barth and Blanke 340; Garland 174)?[15] Only that which comes from God can be such a shadow. Thus, we conclude that 2:16-17 has OT holy occasions and dietary laws in view.[16] Even Rayburn, who says that the Colossian epistle is refuting "a mixture of Jewish ritualism and an Oriental Gnostic-type philosophy," sees Jewish observances in 2:16-17 (83-84).

Paul, however, is not opposing the observance of the food laws and the festivals and days per se. Paul is essentially saying whether one observes the Sabbath (and festivals and dietary laws) or not has to be left to his/her own decision (cf. Rom. 14:5-6; Bruce, *Colossians* 114). The implication then is that Sabbath observance is not mandatory for a Christian; he/she is neither obligated to nor barred from Sabbath observance. No one should judge another based on their observance or nonobservance of the festivals and dietary regulations (see Blomberg, "Sabbath as Fulfilled," *Perspectives* 341f; De Lacey 182-83). In other words, Paul, like Jesus, neither condemns nor requires Sabbath observance. Blomberg rightly states, "There could scarcely be a clearer pair of verses [Col. 2:16-17] proving that Sabbath observance is optional for believers" ("Sabbath as Fulfilled," *Perspectives* 342). In other words, outward observance of OT dietary laws, festivals, and special days, which were the shadow, are dispensable once Christ has appeared (cf. Heb. 10:1).

Moreover, to deduce from the text as the sabbatarians usually do, that dietary laws, annual festivals, and new moon celebrations are not essential but only the Sabbath observance is essential—Saturday or Sunday—in the post-Cross era, is problematical. If Sabbath is mandatory, then all other things mentioned in v. 16 are mandatory as well (cf. Blomberg, "Sabbath as Fulfilled," *Perspectives* 344). To this assertion, the sabbatarians disagree. Such a selective application is improper. The lesson thus concerns the freedom found in Christ from the OT laws including those on food and drink, and festivals and days (cf. Hooker 135-36). None of these are mandatory for Christians.

Romans 14:5-6a; Galatians 4:10-11

In Rom. 14:5-6a, Paul says everyone should themselves decide whether or not to observe special days. No one should judge another based on observance or nonobservance of such days (and on their diet) (vv. 2-6, 10). What "day(s)" is Paul referring

to? More importantly, is the Sabbath included? Some believe
it is not (e.g., MacCarty 31-32; Erdman 143). Murray holds
that *based on the overall Scriptural witness*, Rom.14:5 excludes
the weekly Sabbath and refers only to "the ceremonial holy
days of the Levitical institution" (257-59). As De Lacey has
rightly pointed out, such interpretation is a result of dogmatic
predisposition (194 n. 154). If Jewish holy days are in view,
then the Sabbath, which is probably the most prominent of
the holy days, is certainly included; if it were not, then some
clarification about the exception is to be expected, but none
follow. Bacchiocchi argues that the Sabbath is not included
because Rom. 14:5 concerns fast days, but the Sabbath is a
feast day (*Sabbath to Sunday* 342-44). E. Harrison thinks that "a
special day set apart" for feasting or fasting is in view (146).
However, the abstention and non-abstention from certain food
in the context does not suggest that fast or feast days are in
view; rather it makes a point by drawing a parallel, i.e., just
like one's dietary choice is a matter of his/her conscience, so
is the observance of special days. Thus, the Sabbath is most
probably included in the verse (so also Moo, *Romans*, NICNT
842; Dunn, *Romans 9-16*, 805-06; Byrne 409). However, the
pagan holy day observances are most likely excluded because
Paul would not consider them capable of honoring God (see
v. 6a; cf. Weiss 141).[17] In fact, some believe that the Sabbath is
the real concern here.[18] The existence of the definite article in
v. 6a (τὴν ἡμέραν, "the day") seems to suggest that a particular
day is in view, and in the absence of qualifications, it would
most likely refer to the most prominent of the sacred days,
i.e., the Sabbath (cf. Weiss 143). The message, then, is that it is
an individual decision as to whether or not to observe special
days including the Sabbath (so also De Lacey 182). What is
important is that everything is done "to/for the Lord" (v. 6).

The implication for us is that the Sabbath is not obligatory for Christians.[19]

Gal. 4:10, like Rom.14:5, does not use the word 'Sabbath.' Hence, some believe that the verse refers to pagan observances (e.g., Martin, "Pagan and Judeo-Christian" 111-19) while many believe they are Jewish (e.g., Schreiner 279; McKnight 217; Boice 476; Bruce, *Galatians* 19, 29f, 205-07; Fung 193; Hays 288; Longenecker 182-83). George, while thinking that these refer to Jewish observances, sees the possibility of "double entendre" referring to both Jewish and pagan observances (317 including n. 207; see also Blomberg, "Sabbath as Fulfilled," *Perspectives* 348; Betz 217-18). However, the purpose of the epistle, that of opposing the Judaizers,[20] suggests a Jewish schema. The immediate context (vv. 8-11) might seem to suggest that a return to paganism is in view, but as Schreiner has pointed out, the message of the verses is that subjecting oneself to the OT law is equivalent to reverting to paganism (39, 275, 276, 279; so also Longenecker 181; cf. Hays 288). If this is correct, then the Sabbath is included in the ἡμέρας ("days") of v. 10. The context (vv. 8-11) clearly shows that the observances of v. 10 are condemned, Sabbath included. Nonetheless, the text cannot be taken in isolation to say that Paul condemns Sabbath observance (and/or other religious observances). The broader context of the epistle makes it clear that what Paul is refuting here is these observances when taken to be Christian obligation as though they were required for salvation; he is not opposing their voluntary observance, particularly by the Jewish Christians (cf. Bruce, *Galatians* 29, 205; Fung 193). Similarly, in light of Paul's words in other epistles (e.g., Rom. 14:5-6; Col. 2:16-17) and the overall NT teaching, it is clear that Sabbath and other Jewish observances are neither mandatory nor condemnatory (cf.

George 317). The conclusion, thus, is that Sabbath observance is not binding on Christians.

Hebrews 3:7-4:13

The Sabbath in Hebrews 3:7-4:13 is spiritual and eschatological (see Ross 404-05; Blomberg, "Sabbath as Fulfilled," *Perspectives* 349-51). Two things are crucial here. First, it does not concern the literal observance of the Sabbath. Second, the Sabbath rest here is already entered (4:3) by faith in Christ and yet to be fully entered (4:11). That is, the salvific Sabbath rest of the Hebrews is to be seen from the 'already and not yet' paradigm.[21] The text does not contribute to the discussion of the earthly observance of the Sabbath, weekly or otherwise; it uses the OT Sabbath to point to the spiritual reality brought about by Christ's death and resurrection. The implication is that Christians are not obligated to observe any weekday as special day; the Sabbath is not binding on them.[22] Of course, the text does not condemn Sabbath observance either. The epistle is written to Jewish Christians who most likely observed the Sabbath.

Sabbath for Today

What is the significance of the Sabbath for today? To answer this question, the fact that the NT neither condemns nor mandates literal Sabbath observance should be taken into consideration. Nevertheless, considering the fact that Christianity is an offshoot of Judaism and the early Christians, including the leaders, were predominantly Jews, it is no surprise that the Sabbath (and other Jewish practices) received much attention. The unanimous testimony of the NT, however, is that those who are in Christ are not obligated to observe the Sabbath. Lincoln rightly concludes from his study of the Sabbath in the NT that "the physical rest of the Old Testament Sabbath has become the salvation rest of the true Sabbath" (215). Jesus pronounced that He came to fulfill the law (Mt. 5:17). Therefore, the best way to understand the Sabbath law in the post-Cross era is to see it as fulfilled in Christ just like any other OT law (see Blomberg, "Sabbath as Fulfilled," *Perspectives* 323f; cf. Ross 405-06).[23] However, Jesus also said in that same verse (i.e., Mt. 5:17) that He did not come to abolish the law. The law is fulfilled but not abolished.[24] The meaning of this pronouncement most probably is that the law need not be kept literally but there are principles to be learned and applied to any time and place. When it comes to the Sabbath, there are two principles/concerns that are not mutually exclusive: (1) periodic rest for everyone, and (2) welfare of the poor, (the) vulnerable and (the) marginalized. The next step is to see how these principles can be applied to contemporary situation(s) without being Pharisaic. The Sabbath application for today should not be reduced to a list of dos and don'ts as in the Pharisaic tradition and the Mishnah. We will thus attempt to provide general guidelines alone.

Periodic Rest

The first and the central concern of the Sabbath is periodic rest. In the twenty-first century when people are involved in the "rat race" of achieving more and more, and accumulating more and more, the call to rest is urgent. Although Christians are not bound by the law to observe the Sabbath, its basic principle/concern that humans need periodic rest from their labors is always valid (so also Rooker, *Leviticus* 284). Periodic rest is necessary not merely on theological grounds but on physical and psychological ones as well. How then can we keep the Sabbath according to its spirit and not according to its letter? To answer this question, we have to first understand that resting on the Sabbath does not necessarily mean doing absolutely nothing. There were legitimate activities on the Sabbath even in the OT (see Dressler 33-34; Douma 120).

What then will the Sabbath rest look like today and what are the appropriate activities? Since the primary purpose of observing the Sabbath is to rest and be refreshed (Exod. 23:12, 31:17), Dawn is probably correct: "Activity that is enjoyable and freeing and not undertaken for the purpose of accomplishment (. . .) qualifies as acceptable for Sabbath time" (*Keeping the Sabbath* 5). The Sabbath rest involves abstaining from one's daily activities. Non-routine activities that a person enjoys and which rejuvenate him/her are appropriate. Consider this in terms of work and play.[25] For example, to a professor, reading is normally work but swimming can be play; whereas for a professional swimmer, the reverse may be true. Thus, the idea is not necessarily doing nothing but breaking out of one's normal work rhythm and engaging in something that is rejuvenating, which in turn will provide the vigor to continue with the routine following six days after the Sabbath (cf. Olson 55). Nonetheless, these activities should not be physically and/or mentally so demanding that they take the life and energy out of a person—physical or mental—hindering his/her desire or ability to continue with work in the days following the Sabbath. If this happens, then the whole purpose of the Sabbath rest is lost. Therefore, the activities on the Sabbath should be mild, enjoyable, and minimally demanding (probably there is no activity or "play" that is absolutely non-demanding). The time of rest should not be turned into a "new type of work" or "industry" with activities that soon enslave us (Christensen 119). If one desires not to be involved in any "activity" per se, but chooses non-activity, that is perfectly acceptable, too.

Such a stance should not be seen as laziness or idleness if undertaken with the awareness that it is God's gracious gift to us in the midst of our frantic lives.

I strongly disagree with Stuart that "if one were physically active in pursuit of service to God and/or godly service to others, it would be entirely consistent with the Sabbath law to work hard at such sorts of activities and be reasonably worn out by them at the end of the day" (*Exodus* 460). Firstly, how much wearing out is "reasonable" is not clear. Secondly, resting and being refreshed is the primary purpose of the Sabbath. Of course, following Stuart's advice does not entail breaking the Sabbath because we are not obligated to keep it in the first place. However, if we are living by the Sabbath principle, then his stance is questionable. This assertion is not to deny that attending to pressing needs such as emergencies is necessary. Stuart's statement later in the same work is more appreciable that

> the Sabbath, whether of years or days, was intended by God to provide restoration and well-being for God's people, not merely a cessation of all activity. This perspective is often missed by strict Sabbatarians in modern times, just as in ancient, who stress doing nothing rather than doing what is relaxing and engaging in the least possible physical activity over doing things that produce refreshment and restoration (*Exodus* 530).

A fixed day set aside every week for rest so that one has a proper life rhythm of work and rest is ideal. As such, for most it will be the weekly public holiday (or weekly day off from work). Most people do not have the luxury of choosing their own day of rest. On the more practical side, there might be occasions when one cannot avoid busyness for a longer period of time, and hence there is not enough rest or a weekly day off. Since the Sabbath is not being observed according to the letter of the law, he/she need not be anxious. In such cases, taking a few days off to rest after the completion of the task is advisable. Over-busyness for long periods of time as a regular phenomenon, however, should be avoided. The ideal is one day of rest weekly.

Welfare of the Poor and Vulnerable

The second concern of the Sabbath, which is not absent in the first, is the welfare of the poor. The Sabbath day is humanitarian in that it highlights the need of periodic rest for slaves. The sabbatical and Jubilee years attempt to ensure that the poor and weak are not endlessly exploited by the rich and powerful. Hence, Christian employers are to be careful to avoid exploitation of their employees in any form. The households with house-helps are to treat the latter humanely. Similarly, at a broader level, the Church is called to stand against the exploitation and injustice of the poor and (the) vulnerable in the society. For instance, in the South Asian context, the exploitation of the "labor class"[26] is prominent,[27] not to mention child labor in extreme forms. The Sabbath law invites the church to speak on behalf of these people many of whom do not have even a day off in the week in addition to exceptionally long working-hours daily. God is concerned about the poor and the vulnerable—e.g., the labor class (cf. the slaves)—all having been created in His image. The church should be concerned as well. The church could also apply the Sabbath principle by helping those who are drowned in debt come out of it and start afresh, and by providing housing for the landless and/or homeless. These are a few examples. Each church (and individual Christian) should apply the Sabbath principle based on their own context. Blomberg writes that "working for economic justice in our world is one key form of Sabbath fulfillment" ("Sabbath as Fulfilled," *Perspectives*

351 n. 115). Blomberg is correct. However, working for any form of justice, not merely economic, is part of the Sabbath application/fulfillment.[28]

Corporate Worship?

What about the weekly corporate worship? Our study clarifies that the Sabbath legislation does not require it. However, the weekly worship is crucial, not based on the Sabbath but on other grounds. If we are talking about the Sabbath day, then rest is the agenda, not corporate worship. Nonetheless, there are some bases for corporate worship. First, Heb. 10:25 warns us against failing to gather together. Second, the early church gathered regularly, especially on the first day of the week. Third, gathering together is essential for the spiritual nourishment and well-being of the members of a church. Although these do not require corporate worship to be weekly, it is the most ideal because one day per week as the national holiday is normal worldwide. However, weekly worship service should not be the only time for fellowship among church members; care cells, etc., are also essential.

The application of the Sabbath principle also means that the churches do not clutter the weekly public holiday with so many meetings and programs for the parishioners that the latter are equally or even more wearied at the end of the day than they are in their work-days. The time beyond the corporate worship should be given to the parishioners for rest and refreshing. To admonish the parishioners to attend the corporate worship and to not be anxious when the worship service becomes very lengthy because it is Sabbath—a day set apart for the Lord— while not talking about rest whatsoever, is problematic. This phenomenon is common at least in Nepali churches. Pastors should encourage the parishioners to take the time outside the corporate worship for rest and rejuvenation. They should be encouraged not to continue their busyness of the other six days. Because the church leaders do not emphasize rest in relation to "Sabbath observance" but rather attendance at the worship service, many parishioners are in a haste to finish their "Sabbath duty" by attending the church and catching up with their usual business. What is more, some are multitasking even in the church as Brueggemann has shown (see *Sabbath as Resistance* 58-68). Quite paradoxically in Nepal, where I come from, Christians commonly call the Sabbath day (or weekly holiday) *bishramko din* (lit. day of rest) but I cannot recall any pastor/preacher talking about rest in relation to the day; it is always church attendance.

Sabbath for Clergy

For parishioners, the worship day[29] is the best day because most get only one day off in a week. However, church ministers are the busiest on that day. Everyone needs rest regularly from their labors including "ministry." Burnout in ministry is quite common today.[30] Ministers are not superhuman. Hence, a day off on one of the weekdays is appropriate. Many churches today practice it. Drudge does not approve this idea of taking another day off for rest because he sees Sabbath as a communal exercise. He thus says pastors should also take the worship day to be the Sabbath by minimizing their activities on the day—avoiding counseling parishioners, committee meetings, house visits, etc. (Drudge 11-12). Drudge's suggestion of not making the worship day the busiest for pastors is commendable but that is not always practical. Pastors need to be available for some parishioners on the day of worship because other days are work-days for the latter, particularly in places like

South Asia—and I am speaking from experience—where many parishioners are of "labor class" for whom having a day off on weekdays is next to impossible. Granted that church ministers avoid activities such as meetings and counseling on that day, it still is quite demanding for many. For instance, many churches have multiple worship services on the day. Even if the remainder of the day is given for rest, that is not sufficient. Thus, one of the weekdays set aside for rest is appropriate unless he/she has minimal activities on other days of the week; remember we are not legally bound to observe the Sabbath. The best choice for church ministers is the day following the worship day because the latter is likely his/her most demanding day. Peterson does the same although one might find his practice of the day to be slightly legalistic.[31]

Pastors/ministers should learn to trust in the Lord and not be obsessed with performance. Over-busyness should not be seen as extra piety. Perhaps Tuell is correct:

> "Letting go" is hard for all of us, but perhaps especially for clergy. We are uncomfortable with rest: to us, it smacks of indolence and nonproductivity. . . . Perhaps, however, our feverish need for busyness demonstrates not zeal, but anxiety; our drive to be constantly involved may actually reflect our need to be in control. Sadly, this obsession with effectiveness and efficiency is neither effective nor efficient! Our most productive periods often come when we are not seeking to be productive, when in stillness and calm we open ourselves to new insights, through the moving of the Spirit. We need to stop: to trust God, to trust our congregations, to let go (52).

What better way to make this happen than to observe periodic rest based on the Sabbath principle?

Summary

Our study in this chapter has revealed that the NT neither mandates Sabbath observance nor condemns its non-observance. Since the early Christians and their leaders were predominantly Jews, it is no wonder that the Christians and churches debated the validity of the Sabbath and other OT laws, particularly for gentile Christians. The unanimous testimony of the NT is that Christians are not obligated to observe the Sabbath because the law has been fulfilled in Christ. The law is fulfilled not abolished, which probably means that literal adherence to the law is not necessary while the principles can be learned and applied to any time and place. As such, the Sabbath law is based on two principles/concerns: (1) periodic rest for all, and (2) welfare of the poor. Christians do well to set aside one day of the week as their day of rest to break from their normal routine and be refreshed. For most people it will be the weekly public holiday when a part of the day is given for corporate worship because that is likely the only day they get off in the week. Corporate worship is not to be emphasized based on the Sabbath but is essential on other grounds. Since the clergy are quite busy on the worship day, another day taken off weekly is advisable. Moreover, the Sabbath also invites Christians to behave humanely with those who work for or under them, to speak on behalf of the poor and the vulnerable, to stand for justice and against exploitation. In addition, churches/Christians can elevate the condition of the poor by providing necessary assistance such as helping them pay off their debts.

Endnotes

[1] For the unity of the text, see Stein 142-44.

[2] Although Mark mentions Abiathar, his father Ahimelech was the high priest at the time. For proposed solutions, see Lane 115-16.

³ For varied interpretations of vv. 27-28, see Guelich 123-27.

⁴ For varied interpretations of vv. 25-26, see Guelich 121-23.

⁵ Chreia is a "shrewd" communication and enthymemic chreia "occurs when the chreia is presented as a syllogism with one if [*sic*] its premises missing" (Parsons 59).

⁶ Two other alternatives have been proposed for the translation of vv. 27-28 based on the Aramaic *bar nasha* which can be translated either 'man' or 'son of man.' Beare (130-36), relying on Manson, holds that both the verses should be translated with 'Son of man'; thus, 'The Sabbath was made for the Son of man and not the Son of man for the Sabbath' (v. 27). He thus understands the verses to mean that since the Sabbath was made for the 'Son of man' (i.e., Jesus), and He being the Messiah and the Lord of the Sabbath, has authority over it. Beare sees this text as the early church's apologetic of its Sabbath observance (contra Stein 143-44), and the mention of David as attributing Messiahship to Jesus. Some (e.g., Rordorf 64), on the contrary, hold that both the verses should be translated with 'man' rather than the 'Son of Man/man'; hence, 'so the man is lord even of the Sabbath' (v. 28). Both these suggestions are questionable. The most natural translation, which is what the Greek text also requires, is 'man' in v. 27 and 'Son of Man' in v. 28.

⁷ Dwelling in the matters of authorship is beyond the scope of this study. See the epistle's own claim in 1:1 and 4:18. See O'Brien (xli-xlix) for a discussion of authorship.

⁸ Cf. Vaughan who sees the possibility that "Paul was not thinking of Jewish law at all, but simply of *the peculiar ascetic tendencies of the Colossian heresy*" (203, emphasis mine).

⁹ Dunn (*Colossians* 174) sees here the Jewish group at Colossae being critical of gentile Christians who were not observing the Jewish dietary laws.

¹⁰ Block, however, believes that the "Sabbaths" (plural) here is referring not to the weekly Sabbath but to the non-weekly Sabbaths (*For the Glory* 279). However, the word group festival-new moon-Sabbath(s) suggests that the weekly Sabbath is in view; other Sabbaths are associated with the yearly festivals and are covered by the first category (i.e., ἑορτῆς, festival).

¹¹ See O'Brien xxx-xxxviii for an overview.

¹² The phrase τῶν στοιχείων often translated spiritistically (e.g., "elemental spirits") may not even have spiritistic connotation (e.g., "elemental principles"; cf. NASB, NIV).

[13] Cf. Melick (266-68), who sees an ascetic-type Jewish separatist regulations concerning OT law on dietary and special days represented in this text.

[14] On the use of σῶμα rather than εἰκών ('form, image'), see O'Brien 139-41.

[15] For translations/interpretations of v. 17b (τὸ δὲ σῶμα τοῦ Χριστοῦ) along the lines of 'church' and '(physical) body of Christ,' see Barth and Blanke 340-42 (cf. Lohse, *Colossians* 117). Melick sees "Christ and the new age he inaugurated" as the substance/image (269). Even with these interpretations, our argument stands. MacCarty (29) errs in equating "the regulations of the heresy" with the shadow.

[16] Martin believes that the grammar of 2:16-17 has been misunderstood by virtually all commentators. There is an ellipsis of κρινέτω in the second clause of v. 17 (Martin, "But Let Everyone" 249-55). His translation of the verses (254): "Therefore do not let anyone critique you by *[your or her/his?]* eating and drinking or by *[your or her/his?]* participation in a feast, a new moon, or sabbaths, which things are a shadow of future realities, but *let everyone discern* the body of Christ *by [your or her/his?] eating and drinking or by [your or her/his?] participation in a feast, new moon, or sabbaths, which things are a shadow of future realities.*" This suggestion with so much of filling-in-the-supposed-gaps is very interesting but quite improbable in a non-poetic text.

[17] N. T. Wright, while believing that Jewish festive days are in consideration, allows for the possibility of reference to pagan festive days (736); with the latter, I disagree.

[18] E.g., Weiss 141-42. However, his argument that the debate concerned some considering one day of the week to be the Sabbath while others took all seven days to be so, to which Paul said both were acceptable (142ff), is dubitable. I believe that the debate was whether or not a Christian is obligated to keep the one-in-seven-days Sabbath.

[19] Most probably, the strong are those who consider every day alike whereas the weak consider one day differently (more important) than another (contra De Lacey 182). See Moo, *Romans,* NIVAC 451 for major suggestions on the identification of the strong/weak.

[20] For surveys of the major identifications in the 20th century of the Galatian "troublemakers," see Fung 3-9; Bruce, *Galatians* 23-25; Schreiner 39-47; see also Longenecker lxxxix-xciv. Traditionally it has been held that the troublemakers were Judaizers, namely, those Jewish

Christians who required of the gentile Christians a strict observance of the Mosaic Law. Many scholars still believe this to be true although the troublemakers' precise identification is difficult (e.g., Schreiner 39, 47-49; Fung 7-9; Bruce, *Galatians* 25f; Longenecker xcv-xcvi, 182-83; Boice 476) and I believe that is correct. Martin considers the epistle to be Paul's refutation of Galatian Christians' apostasy and *return to paganism* because they deemed circumcision a requisite of Christianity; and they were not willing to undergo circumcision ("Pagan and Judeo-Christian" 111-19). The suggestion is interesting but not plausible (see Schreiner's refutation of Martin's hypothesis: pp. 37-38).

[21] For a succinct and commendable interpretation of the text, see Lincoln 205-14.

[22] To push the text to say that it requires weekly Sabbath observance (e.g., Grossmann 125-37, who sees σαββατισμός as referring to the weekly Sabbath) is erroneous.

[23] For an overview of major Christian views on the Sabbath, see Swartley 65-90. For a more detailed work in which four scholars present a view each and the other three respond, see *Perspectives on the Sabbath*. Block believes that the Sabbath is transformed rather than terminated or fulfilled in Christ. He compares weekly Sabbath with circumcision and Passover and holds that the seventh-day Sabbath is likely replaced by the first day just as the latter two are replaced by baptism and the Lord's Supper. (He also believes that like the circumcision and Passover the Sabbath is non-cultic and predates the cult.) To his credit, he is non-dogmatic about it and acknowledges that "unlike the rites of baptism and the Lord's Supper, the New Testament never mandates the transformation of the seventh-day Sabbath into a first-day Lord's day, let alone making it a day of assembly" (Block, *For the Glory* 282-83). We maintain that the Sabbath is fulfilled in Christ.

[24] Blomberg is correct: "The appropriate hermeneutical paradigm for Christian interpretation of the law would therefore seem to be as follows. Every passage in the Hebrew Scriptures has some abiding relevance for Christians, but no passage can be properly applied until one understands how it has been fulfilled in Christ" ("Sabbath as Fulfilled," *Sabbath in Jewish* 126).

[25] Work is the activity that is part of one's everyday life (profession); play is something that one enjoys doing without pressures, deadlines, etc.

[26] Although I do not personally like this terminology, I am using it to make the message clearer, which is not communicated well by the related terms, e.g., "working class."

[27] This scenario is not limited to South Asia. For instance, a recent investigation in Malaysia also shows widespread exploitation of the foreign factory workers (see Greenhouse, "Report Cites Forced Labor").

[28] For an example of a modern-day manifestation of international large scale exploitation of the poor, see Appendix 2. Can the church stand against such inhumanity, especially where the church's voice is strong?

[29] I am using "worship day" or "day of worship" rather than "Sunday" because even though Sunday is applicable to the majority, it is not true of every nation in the world. For example, in Nepal, that day is Saturday— the public holiday—and Sunday is the first working day of the week. In Islamic nations, Friday is usually the weekly public holiday. Moreover, although it sounds ironic in the context of my argument in this book, I am using the term "worship day" also to emphasize that weekly gathering for communal worship is important for Christians while maintaining that this assembling for corporate worship does not amount to keeping the Sabbath. (I hope I will not be accused of downplaying the need of weekly corporate worship.) In addition, the Church in general understands this day to be the "worship day" rather than the "rest day"; in other words, the term resonates well with Christians.

[30] For statistics and other helpful information on clergy burnout, see the website by D. Sherman (www.pastorburnout.com).

[31] Pastors will greatly benefit from Peterson's article, "The Pastor's Sabbath" at <http://www.christianitytoday.com/le/topics/soul/sabbath/lclead04-2.html>.

Conclusion

This study has endeavored to investigate the primary concern of Sabbath regulations and their expressions in the OT. The near-consensus assumption in biblical scholarship today that the Sabbath required the Israelites to rest *and worship* on the seventh day has been evaluated by exegetically studying key biblical texts on the subject. The focus of this study has been the weekly Sabbath because it is hotly debated among Christians. However, the study also looked at the sabbatical and Jubilee years to see what light they might shed on Sabbath's primary concern. This study is important because the majority of Christians today believe that they are observing the Sabbath by attending church service while the primary concern of the Sabbath, i.e., rest, has been widely neglected. The study is even more important because we do not want our theology and praxis to be based on faulty assumption(s)—albeit widely held even by the most learned—about what the Bible teaches on any subject.

We began our study by looking at the theories on the origin of the Sabbath and discovered that no satisfactory explanation has been found for the extra-Israelite origin of the institution. The Sabbath is likely of an Israelite origin. More important to us is the issue of what the Sabbath law required of the Israelites. We have discovered that the OT did not require worship from the general populace in Israel on the Sabbath day. Only the priests were involved in cultic activity, which they did on other six days as well. The difference is that on the Sabbath, a double portion was offered on the altar.

Rest is central to the Sabbath; rest for humans and animals (Sabbath day) and rest for the land (sabbatical and Jubilee years). Worship is not required by the Sabbath law. The biblical scholarship has erroneously assumed that the Sabbath day was a day of rest *and worship* for even the non-priestly Israelites. Lev. 23:3 is the main verse cited to argue that the Sabbath involved (corporate) worship for the Israelites. However, we have found that such is not the case. The phrase מִקְרָא־קֹדֶשׁ is usually mistranslated as 'sacred/holy assembly/convocation' but the phrase simply suggests that the day was a sacred occasion. Similarly, שַׁבַּת שַׁבָּתוֹן is often translated 'Sabbath of solemn rest' and taken to argue that the Sabbath involved worship but the phrase refers to a complete cessation of work and hence an absolute rest. The phrase שַׁבָּת לַיהוָה, also used often to support the notion of worship activity on the Sabbath, probably simply means that Sabbath observance honors YHWH.

Many erroneously believe that the Sabbath involved some worship activity—cultus and/or assembly—also because it is said to be holy. The assumption is that if it is to be holy, then it should be marked by some sacred/cultic activity. However, such need not be the case. Rest, as an imitation of God with the acknowledgment that it is His gracious gift to humankind, is in itself sacred. Holiness in the OT has the idea of set-apartness. The Sabbath is set apart as a day of rest—different from other days that are work-days—and it involves imitation of God and is a matter of obedience to His command. This fact makes the day holy, not some "holy" activity.

Some also believe that Hos. 2:11[13] and Isa. 1:13 prove that the Sabbath involved assemblies. The problem in the former verse is with the translation of מוֹעֵד and in the latter with מִקְרָא and עֲצָרָה; these words are often translated as 'assemblies' but מוֹעֵד is better translated as 'appointed times,' מִקְרָא as 'festivals,' and in the context, עֲצָרָה as 'festivities/festivals' in line with מִקְרָא. Thus, none of these verses prove that the Sabbath involved assemblies.

Isa. 66:23 and Ezek. 46:3 do mention worship (חוה) on the Sabbath but these are eschatological texts whose manner and time of fulfillment is a conundrum. In any case, these texts do not reveal the Sabbath practice of the prophets' times and cannot be taken to support that the Sabbath law required some worship activity from the Israelites. The Sabbath required rest, not worship. However, the faulty understanding that the Sabbath required worship from the Israelites has become so dominant that many scholars, against Scriptural evidence, still maintain that worship was part of Sabbath observance. Saying in one breath that the Sabbath was to be a day of 'rest and worship' has become a commonplace. This misplaced understanding is also influenced by the development of synagogues and Sabbath worship in them, most likely in the STP, which retrospectively generated the belief that the law must have required worship on the Sabbath.

The sabbatical and Jubilee years also did not involve cultic or worship activity; the only exception is the reading of the law in the sabbatical year when people gathered to celebrate the festival of tabernacles. The latter was celebrated every year.

The Sabbath is a humanitarian law concerned with the welfare of the poor and vulnerable. The weekly Sabbath ensures that all, especially the slaves and even the household animals, have one day in seven for rest and recuperation. The sabbatical and Jubilee years establish an institutional mechanism to prevent the poor from being endlessly exploited by requiring periodic release of debts and slaves, providing food for the poor and even non-domesticated animals, and requiring the return of the land to the original owner who might have sold it due to poverty. In addition, these years require the land to be left fallow, i.e., allowed rest. The Sabbath law is non-cultic.

The NT is unanimous that Christians are not obligated to observe the Sabbath because the law is fulfilled in Christ. However, Jesus said He came to fulfill the law not to abolish it, which most likely means that the legalistic observance of the law is not required but it still has validity in the post-Resurrection era in its principles. When it comes to the Sabbath, there are two main principles/concerns that are not mutually exclusive: rest for everyone and welfare of the poor. These principles invite every Christian to consider seriously taking a day off weekly for rest and recuperation. For most Christians, this would mean the weekly public holiday. Most probably this day will involve corporate worship at the local church, which is not required by the Sabbath, but is crucial on other grounds. That being the case, the time outside the worship service should be spent in rest or in activities that one enjoys and rejuvenates them. Taking one of the weekdays off, preferably the day after the worship day, is advisable for the clergy. Moreover, Christians and churches live by the Sabbath principle when they are involved in uplifting the situation of the poor and the vulnerable, and in standing against their exploitation and against injustice.

To emphasize church attendance as the Sabbath observance is erroneous. If Sabbath day observance is the subject, then rest is the agenda. No one today debates whether sabbatical and Jubilee years are to be observed; the Sabbath day alone is debated. As such, it is to be a day of rest. Worship as part of Sabbath observance is a development of Second Temple Judaism with the beginnings of the synagogues. By the time of Christ, synagogue worship on the Sabbath had become a given in Judaism. Christianity, being a child of Judaism, adopted from the synagogue practice the weekly corporate worship. Corporate worship is beneficial and essential but is not mandated by the Sabbath legislation. So, what is the primary concern of the Sabbath? Rest!

Prospect

Probably a deeper problem exists. Phrases like "rest and worship" may suggest that the two are mutually exclusive and a dichotomy is created. For many, as seen in chapter 2, non-activity (i.e., rest) is idleness or laziness. Therefore, the Sabbath can be holy only if it involves some holy *activity*. I believe that our understanding of worship has been limited. A mere non-activity per se may not qualify as worship but the one in line with YHWH's command, as an imitation of Him, and with the acknowledgment that it is His gracious gift to His people, surely qualifies as worship. Brueggemann seems to advocate such a broad understanding of worship. He writes while commenting on Exod. 31:12-18, "The main point about sabbath is not worship but the stoppage of work. That fact is noteworthy, especially in this larger text (chaps. 25-31), which is consumed by worship. Such an awareness invites us to rethink the meaning of worship. In this context, worship is God's creation engaged in joyous rest" ("Exodus" 925). Block states, "Those whose employment requires work on the first day of the week[1] can honor God and refresh themselves by setting aside another *day of worship in the form of rest and relaxation*" (*For the Glory* 284, emphasis mine). If I have read him correctly, Block here takes rest and relaxation as worship. However, "rest" does not find a place even in his broad definition—or rather description—of worship (see Appendix 3). Ancient Israelites did not make a sharp distinction between sacred and secular, nor should we. Our sharp sacred-secular division is probably one of the major reasons that have caused us to push ourselves into believing that the Sabbath entailed worship activity because we do not see how rest/non-activity can be sacred. If our understanding of worship is as broad as it should be, then the Sabbath rest in itself is worship; and maybe we can stop saying 'rest and worship' when it comes to the Sabbath and begin saying 'rest as worship.' Until and unless that happens, our study has at the least shown that *rest as an imitation of the Creator with the acknowledgment that it is His gracious gift to us is sacred!*

Endnotes

[1] Block believes that the OT Sabbath day has been replaced by the first day.

Appendix 1

Sabbath in Current Debate

Creation Ordinance or Mosaic Law?

Was the Sabbath established at creation or was it initiated at Mount Sinai? Bacchiocchi, in "Remembering the Sabbath: The Creation-Sabbath in Jewish and Christian History" (69-97), contends that it is a creation ordinance based on God taking rest after the completion of the creation in Genesis. Rayburn believes so, too. He writes in "Should Christians Observe the Sabbath?": "The Sabbath, like the institution of marriage, was given first to the father of the human race, not to Abraham, father of the Jews" (73). Furthermore, "the law existed long before Sinai, having originated in the Garden of Eden (. . .). It was simply codified formally at Sinai" (75). That is, "the Sabbath is a creation ordinance and not one which had its beginning with the giving of the Ten Commandments to Moses at Mt. Sinai" (73).

On the contrary, in *Dictionary of the Old Testament: Pentateuch* (695-706), Barker argues that the Sabbath is not a creation ordinance but a part of the Israelite covenantal laws, i.e., the Mosaic Law. He comes to this conclusion because: (1) Gen. 2 is not a legal text but is a narrative, (2a) no command is given to humans on keeping the Sabbath in the creation account, (2b) Gen. 2:1-3 bears no mention of humans, (3) God's rest on the seventh day communicates that the creation is complete and good; it is not a model of work and rest for humans to follow, (4) the seventh day receives the Sabbath day status only in Exod. 20:11, and (5) God's resting in the creation account is used by Exod. 20 as a "paradigm" for Israel's Sabbath observance (697). Barker is representative of many scholars.

Is Sabbath Observance Mandatory for Christians?

The previous question (i.e., is the Sabbath a creation ordinance or a Sinai law?), although not inherently associated, is often linked with the question of whether the law is mandatory for Christians. Thus, those who believe that the Sabbath is a creation ordinance generally also believe that it is binding on Christians or even all humanity.

Doukhan, in his chapter entitled "Loving the Sabbath as a Christian: A Seventh-day Adventist Perspective," lucidly expounds the position that the Sabbath law is binding on all Christians. According to him, keeping the Sabbath is seen in SDA theology "as a part of the ultimate test of faith and therefore as a sign of holiness" (157).

Reymond, in "Lord's Day Observance: Man's Proper Response to the Fourth Commandment," also advocates strongly for the Sabbath observance for Christians but on the first day (see next section). He believes that "there are five incontrovertible reasons for insisting that, when instituted,

Sabbath observance was intended to be universally and perpetually binding upon all men." The reasons are: (1) it is a creation ordinance, (2) the seven-day week was a norm between Gen. 2:1-3 and Exod. 20:8-10, and Exod. 16 decisively proves that Sabbath command existed prior to the giving of the Mosaic Law, (3) the first word of the Sabbath command in Exod. 20, i.e., "Remember," suggests that it was not a new command but a preexistent one, (4) the Sabbath commandment is a moral law and all the commandments in the Decalogue are universal and perpetual, and (5) when Jesus says, the Sabbath was made for man, it means the whole humankind; when He says that He is the Lord of the Sabbath, it means "the obligation of Sabbath observance by man, for man's good, is as wide and as continuous as is the sphere of His Lordship . . ." (12-14).

Those who believe that the Sabbath is part of the Mosaic Law also generally believe that it is not binding on Christians— either Saturday or any other day. In "Restless until We Rest in God: The Fourth Commandment as Test Case in Christian 'Plain Sense' Interpretation" (29-41), Greene-McCreight holds that the OT should be interpreted in light of the Christ event—Jesus' life, death, and resurrection. Viewed thus, the Sabbath law is not binding on Christians because Jesus has fulfilled the law. It could however be understood in terms of "you have heard it said . . . but I say . . .." For Christians, then, every day is the Sabbath of rest from "sin." She spiritualizes the Sabbath. Hence, there is no need of any particular day of "rest" because rest is not central to the Sabbath but creation, redemption, and eschatology are. To insist on Saturday, Sunday, or any other day as the Sabbath is, says Greene-McCreight, incorrect for Christians.

Similarly, Blomberg, in "The Sabbath as Fulfilled in Christ: A Response to S. Bacchiocchi and J. Primus" (122-28), reasons that neither Saturday nor Sunday as the Sabbath is mandatory for Christians. He believes that the Sabbath has been fulfilled in Christ and also notes, "The New Testament is conspicuous in its explicit reaffirmation of all nine of the Ten Commandments except the Sabbath command" (125). Blomberg, nonetheless, believes that the Sabbath command is "authoritative" for Christians (see 127). His recent and more detailed work on the "fulfillment view" of the Sabbath is found in *Perspectives on the Sabbath: Four Views* under the title "The Sabbath as Fulfilled in Christ" (305-58) in which he maintains that the Sabbath, having been fulfilled in Christ, is not mandatory for Christians; however, every OT command still has relevance and its application should be based on understanding how each law or command has been fulfilled in Christ.

Seventh Day or First Day?

Those who believe that the command to keep the Sabbath is binding on Christians fall into two camps. One holds that the Sabbath has to be observed on the seventh day and the other holds that the day has been shifted to the first day because it is the "Lord's day," the day on which the Resurrection took place. Some call it the Christian Sabbath.

Seventh-day Baptists and Adventists are the primary proponents of the first view, namely, that the seventh day cannot be replaced by any other day. Bacchiocchi is an example. His PhD dissertation published as a book in 1977 under the title *From Sabbath to Sunday: A Historical Investigation of the Rise of Sunday Observance in Early Christianity* is a lengthy discussion of the issue. He argues in the book that the shift from Saturday to Sunday in the church has no biblical basis; rather it occurred due to external factors such as anti-Judaism and sun worship. Among other arguments in "The Seventh-Day Sabbath" (9-72), MacCarty reasons that YHWH made the new covenant with Israel just like the old and not with the nations of the world. However, in the NT era, the church is the "true Israel." Since the Sabbath was a sign of the covenant between YHWH and His people Israel, it continues to be the sign of God's covenant with the 'new covenant Israel,' i.e., the church (58-62).

The insistence on the seventh-day Sabbath observance is primarily motivated by the belief that the Sabbath is a creation ordinance and that it is a moral command being part of the Decalogue which is considered universal and perpetual. The same argument is often used by Sunday sabbatarians—usually called Christian sabbatarians—as well. Pipa, for instance, argues thus in his chapter entitled "The Christian Sabbath" (esp. 119-28). The difference between Saturday sabbatarians and their Sunday counterparts is that the latter insist that the day has been shifted from the seventh to the first, usually called "the Lord's day." For instance, most in the Reformed tradition believe in this shift to the first day. Reymond believes that the Sabbath for Christians is the first day due to three factors: (1) the command should be understood in terms of "other things being equal"; just as God forbade any work on the day but Jesus showed that works of necessity, worship, and mercy were permissible, "sufficient reason [Christ's resurrection] and competent authority [Christ and the apostles] mandated the alteration" of the Sabbath day observance, (2) the OT prophetically anticipated the shift in the day of Sabbath observance to the Resurrection day, and (3) the Sabbath commandment in the Decalogue does not specify seventh day as the day to be remembered; as such the "different contextual reference" necessitated the shift in the day (14-17). Reymond is quite firm on the view that Sunday as the Sabbath day for Christians is normative: "This desacralizing of the day [Sunday] even among Christians is traceable, at least in part, to the widely-held opinion that the Fourth Commandment is not, and has never been, normative for the church, much less the world" (7). He adds that

> wherever the Lord's Day is presumptuously ignored or defiantly desecrated and people absent themselves from corporate worship of the living and true God, there true religious knowledge wanes and, without that, idolatry, immorality, and disrespect for law are spawned (Rom 1:18-32). In short, the result of Sabbath neglect on a wide scale is inevitably national and international paganism and moral perversity (. . .) (20).

Beckwith, in the fourth chapter of *The Christian Sunday: A Biblical and Historical Study* co-authored with Stott, gives thirteen reasons as to why Sunday is the Christian Sabbath day, the NT fulfillment of the OT Sabbath. He writes, "No other day qualifies to be this restored sabbath except the Lord's Day." Furthermore, "[i]t would remain true that the sabbath was the model on which the disciples originally framed the Lord's Day, and that, when viewed in the light of New Testament theology as a whole, the Lord's Day can clearly be seen to be a Christian sabbath—a New Testament fulfilment to which the Old Testament sabbath points forward" (44, 46-47).

On the other hand, in *Sunday: The History of the Day of Rest and Worship in the Earliest Centuries of the Christian Church*, Rordorf, while insisting that Sunday should be the day of worship for Christians, says that the Sabbath is annulled in Christ. Thus, for him, Sunday is not the Christian Sabbath. His insistence on the first day, among other reasons, is based on his belief that Sunday is probably intended by Jesus Himself to be the day for worship since He most probably had evening meals with His disciples on Easter and other Sundays thereafter prior to His ascension, and the early church habitually met on Sunday evenings for celebrating the Lord's Supper (231-37, 302-04). Rordorf holds that 1 Cor. 16:2, Acts 20:7, and Rev. 1:10 are all references to Sunday and hence are proofs of the early church's meeting on Sundays (193-215). Sunday as the day of rest is a development only after the verdict of Constantine in 321 CE when he made Sunday the public holiday in the Roman empire; prior to this it was a day of worship for Christians which was held either early in the morning or late in the evening after supper and the rest of the day was spent in work (154-73, 301).

In *For the Glory of God: Recovering a Biblical Theology of Worship*, we find Block's belief that the OT Sabbath has been replaced by Sunday after the coming of Christ (282-85), yet he states, "It seems more important *that a Sabbath day be observed* than *which Sabbath day is observed*" (284, emphases in the original). Block prefers Sunday but is non-dogmatic about it.

How Should the Sabbath Be Observed?

If the Sabbath is to be observed by Christians, how should this be done? Reymond holds that following the apostolic age, this involves gathering together for corporate worship on Sundays which includes singing, praying, exercising spiritual gifts, reading the Scripture, preaching the Word, taking offerings, and observing the sacraments. In addition, acts of "necessity" and of "mercy" are permitted. The bottom line, says Reymond, is "(1) the recognition of the *distinction* of the day from the other six, and (2) the *concentrated adoration* of the Triune God on that day" (19f, emphases in the original).

Rayburn provides the following suggestions: (1) let the Lord determine your actions for the day, (2) do everything for the Lord's glory and not for self-indulgence and pleasure, (3) rest from routine work, (4) attend church worship services— morning and evening, (5) do not make others work so that you can rest; allow them rest too, (6) be involved in acts of compassion and mercy, and (7) spend a portion of the day in the study of the Word and in prayer (85-86).

Dawn, in *Keeping the Sabbath Wholly: Ceasing, Resting, Embracing, Feasting*, suggests that keeping the Sabbath involves four aspects, as reflected in her title: ceasing, resting, embracing, and feasting, and each of these can be undertaken in various ways.[1]

Endnotes

[1] A summarized version of her thoughts in the book is found in her article "A Systematic, Biblical Theology of Sabbath Keeping."

A Modern-Day Example of International Large Scale Exploitation of the Poor

Abbreviations

BT   biotech

CHRGJ   Center for Human Rights and Global Justice

GM   genetically modified

IMF   International Monetary Fund

MNCs   multinational corporations/companies

NYUSoL   New York University School of Law

There has been a buzz for some time in Indian and international media with the issue of Indian farmers' suicides which is related to Monsanto's GM cotton seeds. It was reported by NYUSoL in 2011 that over 250,000 farmers in India committed suicide in the preceding 16 years (CHRGJ 1). Although farmers committing suicide is not new in

India, the deaths of this magnitude is unprecedented in Indian history. This is one of the examples of the consequences of globalization which has allowed some MNCs to monopolize the world market. This is a form of neocolonialism in which no army or direct political might is used but the rich and the powerful subtly exploit the poor and the weak. Monsanto has lured Indian farmers with the promise of pest-free GM crop. Although the seeds were very expensive, farmers bought them due to the promises of plant health which meant no expenditure on pesticides and also a bumper crop which in turn meant high income. The reality turned out to be quite different. After a period the pests became resistant to the insecticide produced by the plant and the crops suffered. The farmers were compelled to buy Monsanto's pesticides, again at a high cost. Moreover, it is reported that "plants growing from GM seeds need twice as much water as traditional crops" (Pain). So, when the rainfall is not sufficient—as is common in India—the crops fail as Indian agriculture is heavily, often solely, dependent on rainfall. In addition, the farmers need to buy seeds annually as the GM seeds of this year cannot be used in the next year and these seeds cost considerably more than traditional seeds. All these factors led many farmers into bankruptcy, deep debt, and loss of land. Under such dire situation, many committed suicide.[1]

The suicide figures are alarming. Indian Ministry of Agriculture statistics show that over 1000 farmers commit suicide in Maharashtra every month on account of these crop failures, and the region is called "suicide belt" (Pain; Malone). According to NYUSoL, 17,638 farmers committed suicide in 2009, i.e., at the rate of a farmer per half-an-hour; 250,000 took their own lives in 16 years; it is thus considered "the largest wave of recorded suicides in human history" (CHRGJ

1). In *Mail Online* Malone even labels it "The GM Genocide." The highest deaths with respect to Monsanto's GM seeds are among the BT cotton farmers (Gucciardi). Malone goes on to say that, India is being used "as a testing ground for genetically modified crops." The Indian government allowed entry to such MNCs in exchange for IMF loans meant to assist "economic revolution" in the 1980s and 1990s (Malone). Malone concludes his article in these words: "Here in the suicide belt of India, the cost of the genetically modified future is murderously high."

Endnotes

[1] See for more detailed stories Pain; Gucciardi; Malone. However, not everyone agrees that Monsanto and its GM seeds are responsible for farmer suicides (e.g., Abid; Pentland), but the evidences are very strong that majority of the suicides are primarily—though not solely—due to Monsanto's initiatives. The plight of Indian farmers can be viewed in the following videos on YouTube: *100% Cotton Made in India* and *Farmers in India Commit Suicide over GM Cotton; Bt Cotton gets 'Punjab-ed' in India*. The latter of the two is highly informative and is a must-watch.

Appendix 3

Daniel I. Block on Worship

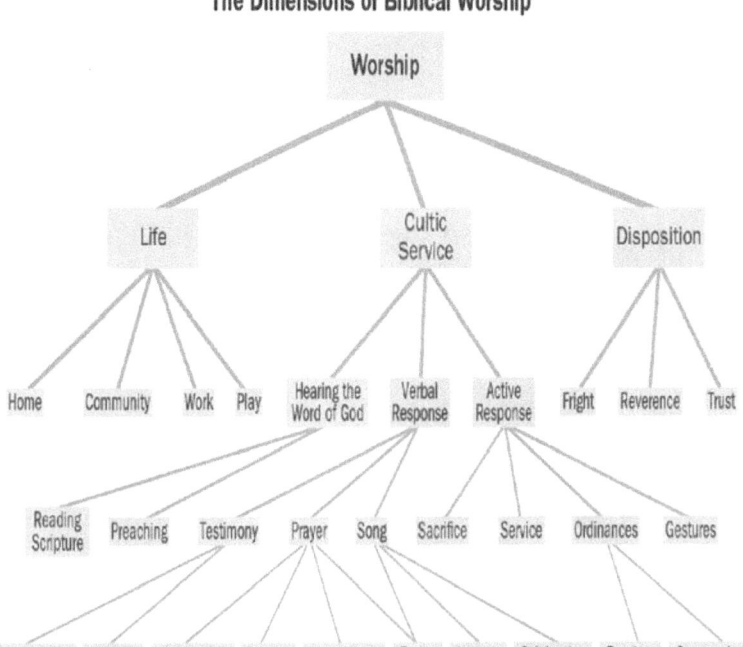

The Dimensions of Biblical Worship

Worship
- Life
  - Home
  - Community
  - Work
  - Play
- Cultic Service
  - Hearing the Word of God
    - Reading Scripture
    - Preaching
    - Testimony
      - Thanksgiving
      - Witness
      - Confession
  - Verbal Response
    - Prayer
      - Petition
      - Intercession
    - Song
      - Praise
      - Lament
  - Active Response
    - Sacrifice
    - Service
      - Celebration
    - Ordinances
      - Baptism
      - Communion
    - Gestures
- Disposition
  - Fright
  - Reverence
  - Trust

Source: Block, *For the Glory of God* 26 fig. 1.4.

Bibliography

Books and Commentaries

Alexander, Ralph H. "Ezekiel." *The Expositor's Bible Commentary*. Ed. Frank E. Gaebelein. Vol. 6. Grand Rapids: Zondervan, 1986. 737-996. Print.

Allen, Ronald B. "Numbers." *The Expositor's Bible Commentary*. Ed. Frank E. Gaebelein. Vol. 2. Grand Rapids: Zondervan, 1990. 657-1008. Print.

Allen, Ronald B., and Gordon L. Borror. *Worship: Rediscovering Missing Jewel*. Portland: Multnomah Press, 1982. Print.

Alt, Albrecht. *Essays on Old Testament History and Religion*. Trans. R. A. Wilson. Oxford: Basil Blackwell, 1966. Print.

Andersen, Francis I., and David Noel Freedman. *Hosea: A New Translation with Introduction and Commentary*. Ed. William Foxwell Albright and David Noel Freedman. Garden City: Doubleday, 1999. Print. The Anchor Bible.

Anderson, G. W. *The History and Religion of Israel*. Oxford: Oxford University Press, 1966. Print. New Clarendon Bible.

Andreasen, Niels-Erik A. *The Old Testament Sabbath: A Tradition-Historical Investigation*. Missoula: Society of Biblical Literature, 1972. Print. SBL Dissertation Series 7.

Ashley, Timothy R. *The Book of Numbers*. Ed. R. K. Harrison. Grand Rapids: Eerdmans, 1993. Print. The New International Commentary on the Old Testament.

Bacchiocchi, Samuele. *From Sabbath to Sunday: A Historical Investigation of the Rise of Sunday Observance in Early Christianity*. Rome: The Pontifical Gregorian University Press, 1977. EBook. 3 Dec. 2013. <http://www.friendsofsabbath. org/Further_Research/Bacchiocchis%20Research/From%20Sabbath%20 to%20Sunday.pdf>.

Bailey, Lloyd R. *Leviticus-Numbers*. Ed. Samuel E. Balentine et al. Macon: Smyth & Helwys, 2005. EBook. Smyth & Helwys Bible Commentary.

Ball, C. J. "The Prophecies of Jeremiah." *The Expositor's Bible*. Ed. W. Robertson Nicoll. Vol. 4. Grand Rapids: Baker, 1982. 5-114. Print. Rpt. of *An Exposition of the Bible*. 1903.

Barth, Markus, and Helmut Blanke. *Colossians: A New Translation with Introduction and Commentary*. Ed. William Foxwell Albright and David Noel Freedman. New York: Doubleday, 1994. Print. The Anchor Bible.

Beckwith, Roger T. *Calendar and Chronology, Jewish and Christian: Biblical, Intertestamental and Patristic Studies*. Boston: Brill, 2001. Print.

Beckwith, Roger T., and Wilfrid Stott. *The Christian Sunday: A Biblical and Historical Study*. Grand Rapids: Baker, 1980. Print. Canterbury Books. Rpt. of *This is the Day*.

Ben Meir, Samuel. *Rashbam's Commentary on Exodus: An Annotated Translation*. Ed. & trans. Martin I. Lockshin. Atlanta: Scholars Press, 1997. Print. Brown Judaic Studies 310.

————, *Rashbam's Commentary on Leviticus and Numbers: An Annotated Translation*. Ed. & trans. Martin I. Lockshin. Providence: Brown Judaic Studies, 2001. Print. Brown Judaic Studies 330.

Betz, Hans Dieter. *Galatians*. Ed. Helmut Koester et al. Philadelphia: Fortress, 1979. Print. Hermeneia: A Critical and Historical Commentary on the Bible.

Blackwood, Andrew W., Jr. *Commentary on Jeremiah*. Waco: Word Books, 1977. Print.

Blenkinsopp, Joseph. *Ezra-Nehemiah: A Commentary*. Ed. Peter Ackroyd et al. Philadelphia: Westminster Press, 1988. Print. The Old Testament Library.

————, *Isaiah 56-66: A New Translation with Introduction and Commentary*. Ed. William Foxwell Albright and David Noel Freedman. New York: Doubleday, 2003. Print. The Anchor Bible.

Block, Daniel I. *The Book of Ezekiel: Chapters 25-48*. Ed. Robert L. Hubbard, Jr. Grand Rapids: Eerdmans, 1998. Print. The New International Commentary on the Old Testament.

————, *For the Glory of God: Recovering a Biblical Theology of Worship*. Grand Rapids: Baker Academic, 2014. Print.

Boccaccini, Gabriele. *Middle Judaism: Jewish Thought, 300 B.C.E. to 200 C.E.* Minneapolis: Fortress, 1991. Print.

Boice, James Montgomery. "Galatians." *The Expositor's Bible Commentary*. Ed. Frank E. Gaebelein. Vol. 10. Grand Rapids: Zondervan, 1976. 409-508. Print.

Breneman, Mervin. *Ezra, Nehemiah, Esther: An Exegetical and Theological Exposition of Holy Scripture*. Ed. E. Ray Clendenen et al. Nashville: Broadman & Holman, 1993. Print. The New American Commentary.

Bright, John. *A History of Israel*. 4th ed. Louisville: Westminster John Knox, 2000. Print.

————, *Jeremiah*. Ed. William Foxwell Albright and David Noel Freedman. Garden City: Doubleday, 1965. Print. The Anchor Bible.

Brooks, James A. *Mark: An Exegetical and Theological Exposition of Holy Scripture*. Ed. David S. Dockery et al. Nashville: Broadman Press, 1991. Print. The New American Commentary.

Brown, Raymond. *The Message of Nehemiah: God's Servant in a Time of Change*. Ed. J. A. Motyer. Leicester: InterVarsity, 1998. Print. The Bible Speaks Today.

_____, *The Message of Numbers: Journey to the Promised Land*. Ed. Alec Motyer. Leicester: InterVarsity, 2002. Print. The Bible Speaks Today.

Bruce, F. F. *The Epistle to the Galatians: A Commentary on the Greek Text*. Ed. I. Howard Marshall and W. Ward Gasque. Grand Rapids: Eerdmans, 1982. Print. The New International Greek Testament Commentary.

_____, *The Epistles to the Colossians, to Philemon, and to the Ephesians*. Ed. F. F. Bruce. Grand Rapids: Eerdmans, 1984. Print. The New International Commentary on the New Testament.

Brueggemann, Walter. "Exodus." *The New Interpreter's Bible: A Commentary in Twelve Volumes*. Ed. David L. Petersen et al. Vol. 1. Nashville: Abingdon Press, 1994. 677-981. Print.

_____, *Sabbath as Resistance: Saying No to the Culture of Now*. Louisville: Westminster John Knox, 2014. Print.

Burtchaell, James Tunstead. *From Synagogue to Church: Public Services and Offices in the Earliest Christian Communities*. Cambridge: Cambridge University Press, 1992. Print.

Byrne, Brendan. *Romans*. Ed. Daniel J. Harrington. Collegeville: Liturgical Press, 2007. Print. Sacra Pagina.

Cairns, Ian. *Word and Presence: A Commentary on the Book of Deuteronomy*. Grand Rapids: Eerdmans, 1992. Print. International Theological Commentary.

Calkins, Raymond. *Jeremiah the Prophet: A Study in Personal Religion*. New York: Macmillan, 1930. Print.

Campbell, Donald K. *Nehemiah: Man in Charge*. Wheaton: Victor Books, 1979. Print.

Carroll, Robert P. *Jeremiah: A Commentary*. Philadelphia: Westminster Press, 1986. Print. The Old Testament Library.

Childs, Brevard S. *The Book of Exodus: A Critical, Theological Commentary*. Ed. Peter Ackroyd et al. Philadelphia: Westminster Press, 1974. Print. The Old Testament Library.

_____, *Isaiah: A Commentary*. Ed. James L. Mays, Carol A. Newsom, and David L. Petersen. Louisville: Westminster John Knox, 2001. Print. The Old Testament Library.

Chirichigno, Gregory C. *Debt-Slavery in Israel and the Ancient Near East*. Ed. David J. A. Clines and Philip R. Davies. Sheffield: JSOT Press, 1993. Print. Journal for the Study of the Old Testament Supplement Series 141.

Christensen, Duane L. *Deuteronomy 1-11*. Ed. David A. Hubbard, Glenn W. Barker, and John D. W. Watts. Dallas: Word Books, 1991. Print. Word Biblical Commentary.

Clements, R. E. *Deuteronomy*. Ed. R. N. Whybray. Sheffield: JSOT Press, 1993. Print. Old Testament Guides.

Clines, David J. A. *Ezra, Nehemiah, Esther*. Ed. Ronald E. Clements. Grand Rapids: Eerdmans, 1984. Print. New Century Bible Commentary.

Cohen, Shaye J. D. *From the Maccabees to the Mishnah*. 2nd ed. Louisville: Westminster John Knox, 2006. Print.

Cole, R. Alan. *Exodus: An Introduction and Commentary*. Ed. D. J. Wiseman. Leicester: InterVarsity, 1973. Print. Tyndale Old Testament Commentaries.

Cole, R. Dennis. *Numbers: An Exegetical and Theological Exposition of Holy Scripture*. Ed. E. Ray Clendenen et al. Nashville: Broadman & Holman, 2000. Print. The New American Commentary.

Cooper, Lamar Eugene, Sr. *Ezekiel: An Exegetical and Theological Exposition of Holy Scripture*. Ed. E. Ray Clendenen et al. Nashville: Broadman & Holman, 1994. Print. The New American Commentary.

Craigie, Peter C. *The Book of Deuteronomy*. Ed. R. K. Harrison. Grand Rapids: Eerdmans, 1976. Print. The New International Commentary on the Old Testament.

Craigie, Peter C., Page H. Kelley, and Joel F. Drinkard, Jr. *Jeremiah 1-25*. Ed. David A. Hubbard, Glenn W. Barker, and John D. W. Watts. Dallas: Word Books, 1991. Print. Word Biblical Commentary.

Criswell, Wallie A. *Isaiah: An Exposition*. Grand Rapids: Zondervan, 1977. Print.

Dawn, Marva J. *Keeping the Sabbath Wholly: Ceasing, Resting, Embracing, Feasting*. Grand Rapids: Eerdmans, 1989. Print.

De Vaux, Roland. *Ancient Israel: Its Life and Institutions*. Ed. Astrid Beck and David Noel Freedman. Trans. John McHugh. 1961. Grand Rapids: Eerdmans, 1997. Print. The Biblical Resource Series.

Donato, Christopher John, ed. *Perspectives on the Sabbath: Four Views*. Nashville: B&H Academic, 2011. Print.

Douma, Jochem. *The Ten Commandments: Manual for the Christian Life*. Trans. Nelson D. Kloosterman. Phillipsburg: P&R Publishing, 1996. Print.

Dozeman, Thomas B. "Numbers." *The New Interpreter's Bible: A Commentary in Twelve Volumes*. Ed. David L. Petersen et al. Vol. 2. Nashville: Abingdon Press, 1998. 1-268. Print.

Driver, S. R. *A Critical and Exegetical Commentary on Deuteronomy*. Ed. Samuel Rolles Driver, Alfred Plummer, and Charles Augustus Briggs. 3rd ed. [c. 1901]. Edinburgh: T&T Clark, 1978. Print. The International Critical Commentary.

Duguid, Iain M. *Ezekiel*. Ed. Terry Muck et al. Grand Rapids: Zondervan, 1999. Print. The NIV Application Commentary.

Dunn, James D. G. *The Epistles to the Colossians and to Philemon: A Commentary on the Greek Text*. Ed. I. Howard Marshall and Donald A. Hagner. Grand Rapids: Eerdmans, 1996. Print. The New International Greek Testament Commentary.

————, *Romans 9-16*. Ed. David A. Hubbard, Glenn W. Barker, and Ralph P. Martin. Dallas: Word Books, 1988. Print. Word Biblical Commentary.

Durham, John I. *Exodus*. Ed. David A. Hubbard, Glenn W. Barker, and John D. W. Watts. Waco: Word Books, 1987. Print. Word Biblical Commentary.

Edersheim, Alfred. *The Temple: Its Ministry and Services*. Updated ed. Peabody: Hendrickson Publishers, 1994. Print.

Enns, Peter. *Exodus*. Ed. Terry Muck et al. Grand Rapids: Zondervan, 2000. Print. The NIV Application Commentary.

Erdman, Charles R. *The Epistle to the Romans: An Exposition*. Philadelphia: Westminster Press, 1925. Print.

Eskenazi, Tamara Cohn. *In an Age of Prose: A Literary Approach to Ezra-Nehemiah*. Ed. Adela Yarbro Collins and P. Kyle McCarter, Jr. Atlanta: Society of Biblical Literature, 1988. Print. Society of Biblical Literature Monograph Series 36.

Fager, Jeffrey A. *Land Tenure and the Biblical Jubilee: Uncovering Hebrew Ethics through the Sociology of Knowledge*. Ed. David J. A. Clines and Philip R. Davies. Sheffield: JSOT Press, 1993. Print. Journal for the Study of the Old Testament Supplement Series 155.

Feinberg, Charles L. "Jeremiah." *The Expositor's Bible Commentary*. Ed. Frank E. Gaebelein. Vol. 6. Grand Rapids: Zondervan, 1986. 357-691. Print.

Fensham, F. Charles. *The Books of Ezra and Nehemiah*. Ed. R. K. Harrison. Grand Rapids: Eerdmans, 1982. Print. The New International Commentary on the Old Testament.

Fishbane, Michael A. *Biblical Interpretation in Ancient Israel*. Oxford: Clarendon Press, 1985. Print.

Flusser, David. *Judaism of the Second Temple Period: The Jewish Sages and Their Literature*. Trans. Azzan Yadin. Vol. 2. Grand Rapids: Eerdmans, 2009. Print.

France, R. T. *The Gospel of Mark: A Commentary on the Greek Text*. Ed. I. Howard Marshall and Donald A. Hagner. Grand Rapids: Eerdmans, 2002. Print. The New International Greek Testament Commentary.

Fung, Ronald Y. K. *The Epistle to the Galatians*. Ed. Gordon D. Fee. Grand Rapids: Eerdmans, 1953. Print. The New International Commentary on the New Testament.

Gane, Roy E. *Leviticus, Numbers*. Ed. Terry Muck et al. Grand Rapids: Zondervan, 2004. Print. The NIV Application Commentary.

Garland, David E. *Colossians and Philemon*. Ed. Terry Muck et al. Grand Rapids: Zondervan, 1998. Print. The NIV Application Commentary.

Gaster, Theodor H. *Festivals of the Jewish Year: A Modern Interpretation and Guide*. New York: William Morrow & Co., 1953. Print.

George, Timothy. *Galatians: An Exegetical and Theological Exposition of Holy Scripture*. Ed. E. Ray Clendenen et al. Nashville: Broadman & Holman, 1994. Print. The New American Commentary.

Gerstenberger, Erhard S. *Leviticus: A Commentary*. Ed. James L. Mays, Carol A. Newsom, and David L. Petersen. Trans. Douglas W. Stott. Louisville: Westminster John Knox, 1996. Print. The Old Testament Library.

Green, James Leo. "Jeremiah." *The Broadman Bible Commentary*. Ed. Clifton J. Allen et al. Vol. 6. Nashville: Broadman Press, 1971. 1-202. Print.

Grogan, Geoffrey W. "Isaiah." *The Expositor's Bible Commentary*. Ed. Frank E. Gaebelein. Vol. 6. Grand Rapids: Zondervan, 1986. 3-354. Print.

Guelich, Robert A. *Mark 1-8:26*. Ed. David A. Hubbard, Glenn W. Barker, and Ralph P. Martin. Dallas: Word Books, 1989. Print. Word Biblical Commentary.

Hailey, Homer. *A Commentary on Isaiah: With Emphasis on the Messianic Hope*. Grand Rapids: Baker, 1985. Print.

Harrelson, Walter J. *The Ten Commandments and Human Rights*. Ed. Walter Brueggemann and John R. Donahue. Philadelphia: Fortress, 1980. Print. Overtures to Biblical Theology.

Harris, R. Laird. "Leviticus." *The Expositor's Bible Commentary*. Ed. Frank E. Gaebelein. Vol. 2. Grand Rapids: Zondervan, 1990. 501-654. Print.

Harrison, Everett F. "Romans." *The Expositor's Bible Commentary*. Ed. Frank E. Gaebelein. Vol. 10. Grand Rapids: Zondervan, 1976. 3-171. Print.

Harrison, R. K. *Leviticus: An Introduction and Commentary*. Ed. D. J. Wiseman. Leicester: InterVarsity, 1980. Print. Tyndale Old Testament Commentaries.

————, *Numbers*. Ed. Kenneth L. Barker. Chicago: Moody Press, 1990. Print. The Wycliffe Exegetical Commentary.

Hartley, John E. *Leviticus*. Ed. David A. Hubbard, Glenn W. Barker, and John D. W. Watts. Dallas: Word Books, 1992. Print. Word Biblical Commentary.

Hays, Richard B. "Galatians." *The New Interpreter's Bible: A Commentary in Twelve Volumes*. Ed. Leander E. Keck et al. Vol. 11. Nashville: Abingdon Press, 2000. 183-348. Print.

Hill, Andrew E. *Enter His Courts with Praise!: Old Testament Worship for the New Testament Church*. 2nd paperback ed. Grand Rapids: Baker, 1996. Print.

Holladay, William L. *Jeremiah 1*. Ed. Paul D. Hanson. Philadelphia: Fortress, 1986. Print. Hermeneia: A Critical and Historical Commentary on the Bible.

Hooker, Morna D. *From Adam to Christ: Essays on Paul*. Cambridge: Cambridge University Press, 1990. Print.

Houtman, Cornelis. *Exodus*. Ed. Cornelis Houtman et al. Trans. Sierd Woudstra. Vol. 2. Kampen: Kok Publishing House, 1996. Print. Historical Commentary on the Old Testament.

———, *Exodus*. Ed. Cornelis Houtman et al. Trans. Sierd Woudstra. Vol. 3. Leuven: Peeters, 2000. Print. Historical Commentary on the Old Testament.

Huey, F. B., Jr. *Jeremiah, Lamentations: An Exegetical and Theological Exposition of Holy Scripture*. Ed. E. Ray Clendenen et al. Nashville: Broadman Press, 1993. Print. The New American Commentary.

Hyatt, James Philip, and Stanley Romaine Hopper. "Jeremiah." *The Interpreter's Bible*. Ed. George Arthur Buttrick et al. Vol. 5. Nashville: Abingdon Press, 1956. 777-1142. Print.

Hyatt, James Philip. *Exodus*. Ed. R. E. Clements. Revised softback ed. Grand Rapids: Eerdmans, 1980. Print. New Century Bible Commentary.

Jensen, Irving L. *Numbers: Journey to God's Rest-Land*. Chicago: Moody Press, 1964. Print.

Jenson, Philip Peter. *Graded Holiness: A Key to the Priestly Conception of the World*. Ed. David J. A. Clines and Philip R. Davies. Sheffield: JSOT Press, 1992. Print. Journal for the Study of the Old Testament Supplement Series 106.

Kaiser, Otto. *Isaiah 1-12: A Commentary*. Ed. Peter Ackroyd et al. Trans. John Bowden. 2nd ed. Philadelphia: Westminster Press, 1983. Print. The Old Testament Library.

Kaiser, Walter C., Jr. "Exodus." *The Expositor's Bible Commentary*. Ed. Frank E. Gaebelein. Vol. 2. Grand Rapids: Zondervan, 1990. 287-497. Print.

———, "Leviticus." *The New Interpreter's Bible: A Commentary in Twelve Volumes*. Ed. David L. Petersen et al. Vol. 1. Nashville: Abingdon Press, 1994. 985-1191. Print.

Kidner, Derek. *The Message of Jeremiah*. Ed. J. A. Motyer. Leicester: InterVarsity, 1987. Print. The Bible Speaks Today.

Kiuchi, Nobuyoshi. *Leviticus*. Ed. David W. Baker and Gordon J. Wenham. Nottingham: Apollos, 2007. Print. Apollos Old Testament Commentary.

Klein, Ralph W. "Ezra and Nehemiah." *The New Interpreter's Bible: A Commentary in Twelve Volumes*. Ed. David L. Petersen et al. Vol. 3. Nashville: Abingdon Press, 1999. 663-851. Print.

Knierim, Rolf P., and George W. Coats. *Numbers*. Ed. Rolf P. Knierim, Gene M. Tucker, and Marvin A. Sweeney. Grand Rapids: Eerdmans, 2005. Print. The Forms of the Old Testament Literature.

Laetsch, Theodore. *Minor Prophets*. St. Louis: Concordia Publishing House, 1956. Print. Concordia Classic Commentary Series.

Lane, William L. *The Gospel of Mark*. Ed. Gordon D. Fee. Grand Rapids: Eerdmans, 1974. Print. The New International Commentary on the New Testament.

Leclerc, Thomas L. *Yahweh Is Exalted in Justice: Solidarity and Conflict in Isaiah.* Minneapolis: Fortress, 2001. Print.

Lee, Francis Nigel. *The Covenantal Sabbath: The Weekly Sabbath Scripturally and Historically Considered.* London: Lord's Day Observance Society, 1969. Print.

Levine, Baruch A. *Leviticus.* Ed. Nahum M. Sarna and Chaim Potok. Philadelphia: The Jewish Publication Society, 1989. Print. The JPS Torah Commentary.

————, *Numbers 1-20: A New Translation with Introduction and Commentary.* Ed. William Foxwell Albright and David Noel Freedman. New York: Doubleday, 1993. Print. The Anchor Bible.

Lohse, Eduard. *Colossians and Philemon.* Ed. Helmut Koester. Trans. William R. Poehlmann and Robert J. Karris. Philadelphia: Fortress, 1971. Print. Hermeneia: A Critical and Historical Commentary on the Bible.

Longenecker, Richard N. *Galatians.* Ed. David A. Hubbard, Glenn W. Barker, and Ralph P. Martin. Dallas: Word Books, 1990. Print. Word Biblical Commentary.

Longman, Tremper, III. *Jeremiah, Lamentations.* Ed. Robert L. Hubbard, Jr. and Robert K. Johnston. Peabody: Hendrickson, 2008. Print. New International Biblical Commentary.

Lundbom, Jack R. *Jeremiah 1-20: A New Translation with Introduction and Commentary.* Ed. William Foxwell Albright and David Noel Freedman. New York: Doubleday, 1999. Print. The Anchor Bible.

Macintosh, A. A. *Hosea.* Ed. J. A. Emerton, C. E. B. Cranfield, and G. N. Stanton. Edinburgh: T&T Clark, 1997. Print. The International Critical Commentary.

Mays, James Luther. *Hosea: A Commentary.* Ed. G. Ernest Wright et al. Philadelphia: Westminster Press, 1969. Print. The Old Testament Library.

McConville, J. Gordon. *Deuteronomy.* Ed. David W. Baker and Gordon J. Wenham. Nottingham: Apollos, 2002. Print. Apollos Old Testament Commentary.

McKane, William. *Jeremiah.* Ed. J. A. Emerton and C. E. B. Cranfield. Vol. 1. Edinburgh: T&T Clark, 1986. Print. The International Critical Commentary.

McKay, Heather A. *Sabbath and Synagogue: The Question of Sabbath Worship in Ancient Judaism.* Boston: Brill Academic, 2001. Print.

McKnight, Scot. *Galatians.* Ed. Terry Muck et al. Grand Rapids: Zondervan, 1995. Print. The NIV Application Commentary.

Melick, Richard R., Jr. *Philippians, Colossians, Philemon: An Exegetical and Theological Exposition of Holy Scripture.* Ed. David S. Dockery et al. Nashville: Broadman Press, 1991. Print. The New American Commentary.

Merrill, Eugene H. *Deuteronomy: An Exegetical and Theological Exposition of Holy Scripture.* Ed. E. Ray Clendenen et al. Nashville: Broadman & Holman, 1994. Print. The New American Commentary.

Milgrom, Jacob. *Leviticus 1-16: A New Translation with Introduction and Commentary.* Ed. William Foxwell Albright and David Noel Freedman. New York: Doubleday, 1991. Print. The Anchor Bible.

_____, *Leviticus 23-27: A New Translation with Introduction and Commentary*. Ed. William Foxwell Albright and David Noel Freedman. New York: Doubleday, 2001. Print. The Anchor Bible.

_____, *Numbers*. Ed. Nahum M. Sarna and Chaim Potok. Philadelphia: Jewish Publication Society, 1989. Print. The JPS Torah Commentary.

Miller, Patrick D. *Deuteronomy*. Ed. James Luther Mays and Patrick D. Miller. Louisville: John Knox Press, 1990. Print. Interpretation.

_____, *The Ten Commandments*. Ed. Patrick D. Miller et al. Louisville: Westminster John Knox, 2009. Print. Interpretation.

Millgram, Abraham E. *Jewish Worship*. Philadelphia: The Jewish Publication Society of America, 1971. Print.

Moo, Douglas J. *The Epistle to the Romans*. Ed. Gordon D. Fee. Grand Rapids: Eerdmans, 1996. Print. The New International Commentary on the New Testament.

_____, *Romans*. Ed. Terry Muck et al. Grand Rapids: Zondervan, 2000. Print. The NIV Application Commentary.

Moore, George Foot. *Judaism in the First Centuries of the Christian Era: The Age of Tannaim*. 3 vols. Peabody: Hendrickson Publishers, 1997. Print.

Motyer, J. A. *The Prophecy of Isaiah*. Leicester: InterVarsity, 1993. Print.

Murphy, Frederick James. *Early Judaism: The Exile to the Time of Jesus*. Peabody: Hendrickson, 2002. Print.

Murray, John. *The Epistle to the Romans*. Ed. F. F. Bruce. One vol. ed. Grand Rapids: Eerdmans, 1968. Print. The New International Commentary on the New Testament.

Myers, Jacob M. *Ezra-Nehemiah: A New Translation with Introduction and Commentary*. Ed. William Foxwell Albright and David Noel Freedman. New York: Doubleday, 1965. Print. The Anchor Bible.

Nelson, Richard D. *Deuteronomy: A Commentary*. Ed. James L. Mays, Carol A. Newsom, and David L. Petersen. Louisville: Westminster John Knox, 2002. Print. The Old Testament Library.

Neusner, Jacob. *The Mishnah: A New Translation*. New Haven: Yale University Press, 1988. Print.

Noth, Martin. *Exodus: A Commentary*. Ed. G. Ernest Wright et al. Trans. J. S. Bowden. Philadelphia: Westminster Press, 1962. Print. The Old Testament Library.

_____, *Leviticus: A Commentary*. Trans. J. E. Anderson. Rev. ed. Philadelphia: Westminster Press, 1977. Print. The Old Testament Library.

_____, *Numbers: A Commentary*. Ed. G. Ernest Wright et al. Trans. James D. Martin. Philadelphia: Westminster Press, 1968. Print. The Old Testament Library.

O'Brien, Peter T. *Colossians, Philemon*. Ed. David A. Hubbard, Glenn W. Barker, and Ralph P. Martin. Waco: Word Books, 1982. Print. Word Biblical Commentary.

Oswalt, John N. *The Book of Isaiah: Chapters 1-39.* Ed. R. K. Harrison. Grand Rapids: Eerdmans, 1986. Print. The New International Commentary on the Old Testament.

———, *The Book of Isaiah: Chapters 40-66.* Ed. Robert L. Hubbard, Jr. Grand Rapids: Eerdmans, 1998. Print. The New International Commentary on the Old Testament.

Owens, John Joseph. "Numbers." *The Broadman Bible Commentary.* Ed. Clifton J. Allen et al. Vol. 2. Nashville: Broadman Press, 1970. 75-174. Print.

Packer, J. I. *Keeping the Ten Commandments.* Wheaton: Crossway Books, 2007. EBook. Rpt. of *I Want to be A Christian.*

Robinson, Gnana. *The Origin and Development of the Old Testament Sabbath: A Comprehensive Exegetical Approach.* Bangalore: UTC, 1998. Print.

Rooker, Mark F. *Leviticus: An Exegetical and Theological Exposition of Holy Scripture.* Ed. E. Ray Clendenen et al. Nashville: Broadman & Holman, 2000. Print. The New American Commentary.

Rordorf, Willy. *Sunday: The History of the Day of Rest and Worship in the Earliest Centuries of the Christian Church.* Trans. A. A. K. Graham. London: SCM Press, 1968. Print.

Ross, Allen P. *Holiness to the Lord: A Guide to the Exposition of the Book of Leviticus.* Grand Rapids: Baker, 2002. Print.

Sarna, Nahum M. *Exodus.* Ed. Nahum M. Sarna and Chaim Potok. Philadelphia: The Jewish Publication Society, 1991. Print. The JPS Torah Commentary.

Schreiner, Thomas R. *Galatians.* Ed. Clinton E. Arnold et al. Grand Rapids: Zondervan, 2010. Print. Zondervan Exegetical Commentary on the New Testament.

Scott, J. Julius, Jr. *Jewish Backgrounds of the New Testament.* Grand Rapids: Baker, 2000. Print. Rpt. of *Customs and Controversies: Intertestamental Jewish Backgrounds of the New Testament.* 1995.

Shao, Joseph Too, and Rosa Ching Shao. *Ezra-Nehemiah.* Ed. Bruce J. Nicholls et al. Singapore: Asia Theological Association, 2007. Print. Asia Bible Commentary Series.

Stein, Robert H. *Mark.* Ed. Robert W. Yarbrough and Robert H. Stein. Grand Rapids: Baker Academic, 2008. Print. Baker Exegetical Commentary on the New Testament.

Stuart, Douglas K. *Exodus: An Exegetical and Theological Exposition of Holy Scripture.* Ed. E. Ray Clendenen et al. Nashville: Broadman & Holman, 2006. Print. The New American Commentary.

———, *Hosea-Jonah.* Ed. Bruce M. Metzger, John D. W. Watts, and James W. Watts. Waco: Word Books, 1987. Print. Word Biblical Commentary.

Swartley, Willard M. *Slavery, Sabbath, War, and Women: Case Issues in Biblical Interpretation.* Scottdale: Herald Press, 1983. Print.

Thompson, J. A. *The Book of Jeremiah.* Ed. R. K. Harrison. Grand Rapids: Eerdmans, 1980. Print. The New International Commentary on the Old Testament.

_____, *Deuteronomy: An Introduction and Commentary.* Ed. D. J. Wiseman. Downers Grove: InterVarsity, 1974. Print. Tyndale Old Testament Commentaries.

Tigay, Jeffrey H. *Deuteronomy.* Ed. Nahum M. Sarna and Chaim Potok. Philadelphia: The Jewish Publication Society, 1996. Print. The JPS Torah Commentary.

Van Seters, John. *The Pentateuch: A Social-Science Commentary.* Ed. Diana J. V. Edelman and Brian B. Schmidt. Sheffield: Sheffield Academic Press, 1999. Print. Trajectories 1.

Vaughan, Curtis. "Colossians." *The Expositor's Bible Commentary.* Ed. Frank E. Gaebelein. Vol. 11. Grand Rapids: Zondervan, 1981. 163-226. Print.

Von Rad, Gerhard. *Deuteronomy: A Commentary.* Ed. G. Ernest Wright et al. Trans. Dorothea Barton. Philadelphia: Westminster Press, 1966. Print. The Old Testament Library.

Waltke, Bruce K., and M. O'Connor. *An Introduction to Biblical Hebrew Syntax.* Winona Lake: Eisenbrauns, 1990. Print.

Walvoord, John F. *The Final Drama: 14 Keys to Understanding the Prophetic Scriptures.* Grand Rapids: Kregel, 1993. 1st Indian ed. Secunderabad: OM-Authentic Books, 2000. Print.

Watson, Robert A. "Numbers." *The Expositor's Bible.* Ed. W. Robertson Nicoll. Vol. 1. Grand Rapids: Baker, 1982. 383-486. Print. Rpt. of *An Exposition of the Bible.* 1903.

Weber, Max. *Ancient Judaism.* Ed. & trans. Hans H. Gerth and Don Martindale. Glencoe: The Free Press, 1952. Print.

Wenham, Gordon J. *The Book of Leviticus.* Ed. R. K. Harrison. Grand Rapids: Eerdmans, 1979. Print. The New International Commentary on the Old Testament.

_____, *Numbers: An Introduction and Commentary.* Ed. D. J. Wiseman. Leicester: InterVarsity, 1981. Print. Tyndale Old Testament Commentaries.

Whybray, R. Norman. *Introduction to the Pentateuch.* Grand Rapids: Eerdmans, 1995. Print.

_____, *The Second Isaiah.* Ed. R. N. Whybray. Sheffield: Sheffield Academic, 1995. Print. Old Testament Guides.

Williamson, H. G. M. *Ezra and Nehemiah.* Ed. R. N. Whybray. Sheffield: Sheffield Academic Press, 1996. Print. Old Testament Guides.

_____, *Ezra-Nehemiah.* Ed. David A. Hubbard, Glenn W. Barker, and John D. W. Watts. Vol. 16. Waco: Word Books, 1985. Print. Word Biblical Commentary.

Williamson, Lamar, Jr. *Mark*. Ed. James Luther Mays and Paul J. Achtemeier. Louisville: John Knox Press, 1983. Print. Interpretation: A Bible Commentary for Teaching and Preaching.

Williamson, Paul R. *Sealed with an Oath: Covenant in God's Unfolding Purpose*. Ed. D. A. Carson. Downers Grove: InterVarsity, 2007. Print. New Studies in Biblical Theology 23.

Wood, Leon J. "Hosea." *The Expositor's Bible Commentary*. Ed. Frank E. Gaebelein. Vol. 7. Grand Rapids: Zondervan, 1985. 161-225. Print.

Wright, Christopher J. H. *The Message of Ezekiel: A New Heart and a New Spirit*. Ed. Alec Motyer. Leicester: InterVarsity, 2001. Print. The Bible Speaks Today.

Wright, N. T. "Romans." *The New Interpreter's Bible: A Commentary in Twelve Volumes*. Ed. Leander E. Keck et al. Vol. 10. Nashville: Abingdon Press, 2002. 395-770. Print.

Youngblood, Ronald F. *The Book of Isaiah: An Introductory Commentary*. 2nd ed. Grand Rapids: Baker, 1993. Print.

Zimmerli, Walther. *Ezekiel 2*. Ed. Paul D. Hanson and Leonard Jay Greenspoon. Trans. James D. Martin. Philadelphia: Fortress, 1983. Print. Hermeneia: A Critical and Historical Commentary on the Bible.

Articles

Asher, Jeffrey R. "The Colossian Heresy: An Ecclesiastical Paradigm?" *Proceedings* 30 (2010): 107-22. *Ebscohost*. Web. 5 September 2014.

Bacchiocchi, Samuele. "Remembering the Sabbath: The Creation-Sabbath in Jewish and Christian History." *The Sabbath in Jewish and Christian Traditions*. Ed. Tamara C. Eskenazi, Daniel J. Harrington, and William H. Shea. New York: Crossroad, 1991. 69-97. Print.

Baden, Joel S. "The Original Place of the Priestly Manna Story in Exodus 16." *Zeitschrift für die alttestamentliche Wissenschaft* 122.4 (2010): 491-504. *Ebscohost*. Web. 21 May 2014.

Baker, David W. "Source Criticism." *Dictionary of the Old Testament: Pentateuch*. Ed. T. Desmond Alexander and David W. Baker. Downers Grove: InterVarsity, 2003. 798-805. Print.

Barker, Paul A. "Sabbath, Sabbatical Year, Jubilee." *Dictionary of the Old Testament: Pentateuch*. Ed. T. Desmond Alexander and David W. Baker. Downers Grove: InterVarsity, 2003. 695-706. Print.

Bass, Dorothy C. "Christian Formation in and for Sabbath Rest." *Interpretation* 59.1 (2005): 25-37. *Ebscohost*. Web. 2 April 2014.

Beare, F. W. "Sabbath Was Made for Man?" *Journal of Biblical Literature* 79.2 (1960): 130-36. *Ebscohost*. Web. 26 August 2014.

Bergsma, John S. "Once Again, the Jubilee, Every 49 or 50 Years?" *Vetus Testamentum* 55.1 (2005): 121-25. *Ebscohost*. Web. 2 April 2014.

Beuken, W. A. M. "Exodus 16:5, 23: A Rule Regarding the Keeping of the Sabbath?" *Journal for the Study of the Old Testament* 32 (1985): 3-14. *Ebscohost*. Web. 22 May 2014.

Blomberg, Craig L. "The Sabbath as Fulfilled in Christ." *Perspectives on the Sabbath: Four Views*. Ed. Christopher John Donato. Nashville: B&H Academic, 2011. 305-58. Print.

—————, "The Sabbath as Fulfilled in Christ: A Response to S. Bacchiocchi and J. Primus." *The Sabbath in Jewish and Christian Traditions*. Ed. Tamara C. Eskenazi, Daniel J. Harrington, and William H. Shea. New York: Crossroad, 1991. 122-28. Print.

Bosman, Hendrik L. "Sabbath." *New International Dictionary of Old Testament Theology and Exegesis*. 1997 ed. Vol. 4. 1157-62. Print.

Bright, John. "The Date of the Prose Sermons of Jeremiah." *Journal of Biblical Literature* 70.1 (1951): 15-35. *Ebscohost*. Web. 17 June 2014.

Budde, Karl. "The Sabbath and the Week: Their Origin and Their Nature." *The Journal of Theological Studies* 30 (1928): 1-15. Print.

Burnside, Jonathan. "'What Shall We Do with the Sabbath-Gatherer?' A Narrative Approach to a 'Hard Case' in Biblical Law (Numbers 15:32-36)." *Vetus Testamentum* 60.1 (2010): 45-62. *Ebscohost*. Web. 6 June 2014.

Casperson, Lee W. "Sabbatical, Jubilee, and the Temple of Solomon." *Vetus Testamentum* 53.3 (2003): 283-96. *Ebscohost*. Web. 2 April 2014.

Chan, Michael J. "Isaiah 65-66 and the Genesis of Reorienting Speech." *Catholic Biblical Quarterly* 72.3 (2010): 445-63. *Ebscohost*. Web. 5 July 2014.

Clines, David J. A. "Nehemiah 10 as an Example of Early Jewish Biblical Exegesis." *Journal for the Study of the Old Testament* 21 (1981): 111-17. *Ebscohost*. Web. 23 June 2014.

Davies, W. D. "Church and Synagogue." *Christianity and Crisis* 24.20 (1964): 235-39. *Ebscohost*. Web. 5 May 2014.

Davis, Ellen F. "Sabbath: The Culmination of Creation." *Living Pulpit* 7.2 (1998): 6-7. *Ebscohost*. Web. 2 April 2014.

Dawn, Marva J. "A Systematic, Biblical Theology of Sabbath Keeping." *The Sabbath in Jewish and Christian Traditions*. Ed. Tamara C. Eskenazi, Daniel J. Harrington, and William H. Shea. New York: Crossroad, 1991. 176-92. Print.

De Lacey, D. R. "The Sabbath/Sunday Question and the Law in the Pauline Corpus." *From Sabbath to Lord's Day: A Biblical, Historical, and Theological Investigation*. Ed. D. A. Carson. Grand Rapids: Academie Books, 1982. 159-95. Print.

Doukhan, Jacques B. "Loving the Sabbath as a Christian: A Seventh-Day Adventist Perspective." *The Sabbath in Jewish and Christian Traditions*. Ed. Tamara C.

Eskenazi, Daniel J. Harrington, and William H. Shea. New York: Crossroad, 1991. 149-68. Print.

Dressler, Harold H. P. "The Sabbath in the Old Testament." *From Sabbath to Lord's Day: A Biblical, Historical, and Theological Investigation.* Ed. D. A. Carson. Grand Rapids: Academie Books, 1982. 21-41. Print.

Drudge, Kevin R. "Living by the Sign of the Sabbath." *Vision* 6.2 (2005): 6-13. *Ebscohost.* Web. 2 April 2014.

Ellison, H. L. "Hebrew Slave: A Study in Early Israelite Society." *Evangelical Quarterly* 45.1 (1973): 30-35. Web. 24 July 2014. <http://biblicalstudies.gospelstudies.org.uk/pdf/eq/1973-1_030.pdf>.

Ferris, Paul Wayne, Jr. "The Manna Narrative of Exodus 16:1-10." *Journal of the Evangelical Theological Society* 18.3 (1975): 191-99. *Ebscohost.* Web. 21 May 2014.

Filson, Floyd V. "The Significance of the Temple in the Ancient Near East, Part IV-Temple, Synagogue, and Church." *Biblical Archaeologist* 7.4 (1944): 77-88. *Ebscohost.* Web. 5 May 2014.

Fredericks, Daniel C. "נֶפֶשׁ." *New International Dictionary of Old Testament Theology and Exegesis.* Vol. 3. 1996 ed. 133-34. Print.

Geller, Stephen A. "Manna and Sabbath: A Literary-Theological Reading of Exodus 16." *Interpretation* 59.1 (2005): 5-16. *Ebscohost.* Web. 2 April 2014.

Gevirtz, Stanley. "New Look at an Old Crux: Amos 5:26." *Journal of Biblical Literature* 87.3 (1968): 267-76. *Ebscohost.* Web. 3 May 2014.

Gladson, Jerry A. "Jeremiah 17:19-27: A Rewriting of the Sinaitic Code?" *Catholic Biblical Quarterly* 62.1 (2000): 33-40. *Ebscohost.* Web. 17 June 2014.

Gordon, Cyrus H. "The Biblical Sabbath: Its Origin and Observance in the Ancient Near East." *Judaism* 31.1 (1982): 12-16. *Ebscohost.* Web. 15 May 2014.

Greene-McCreight, Kathryn. "Restless until We Rest in God: The Fourth Commandment as Test Case in Christian 'Plain Sense' Interpretation." *Ex Auditu* 11 (1995): 29-41. *Ebscohost.* Web. 2 April 2014.

Grossmann, Robert. "The Sabbath of Hebrews 4:9." *Mid-America Journal of Theology* 2.2 (1986): 125-37. *Ebscohost.* Web. 30 August 2014.

Haag, E. "שַׁבָּת." *Theological Dictionary of the Old Testament.* 2004 ed. Vol. 14. 387-97. Print.

Hallo, William W. "New Moons and Sabbaths: A Case-Study in the Contrastive Approach." *Hebrew Union College Annual* 48 (1977): 1-18. *Ebscohost.* Web. 3 May 2014.

Hamilton, Victor P. "שָׁבַת." *Theological Wordbook of the Old Testament.* 1980 ed. 902-03. Print.

Hasel, Gerhard F. "Sabbath." *The Anchor Bible Dictionary.* Ed. David Noel Freedman et al. Vol. 5. New York: Doubleday. 849-56. Print.

Hicks, Olan L. "The Hebrew Sabbath." *Restoration Quarterly* 3.1 (1959): 23-35. *Ebscohost*. Web. 12 May 2014.

Hicks, Robert Lansing. "The Jewish Background to the New Testament Doctrine of the Church." *Anglican Theological Review* 30.2 (1948): 107-17. *Ebscohost*. Web. 16 May 2014.

Hoenig, Sidney B. "Sabbatical Years and the Year of Jubilee." *Jewish Quarterly Review* 59.3 (1969): 222-36. *JSTOR*. Web. 14 August 2014.

Holladay, William L. "A Fresh Look at 'Source B' and 'Source C' in Jeremiah." *Vetus Testamentum* 25 (1975): 394-412. *Ebscohost*. Web. 17 June 2014.

House, Paul R. "Creation in Old Testament Theology." *Southern Baptist Journal of Theology* 5.3 (2001): 4-17. Web. 3 June 2014. <http://www.sbts.edu/media/publications/sbjt/sbjt_2001fall2.pdf>.

Hubbard, Robert L., Jr. "The Go'el in Ancient Israel: Theological Reflections on an Israelite Institution." *Bulletin for Biblical Research* 1 (1991): 3-19. *Ebscohost*. Web. 12 August 2014.

Jastrow, Morris, Jr. "The Original Character of the Hebrew Sabbath." *The American Journal of Theology* 2.2 (1898): 312-52. *JSTOR*. Web. 12 May 2014.

Kahn, Pinchas. "The Expanding Perspectives of the Sabbath." *Jewish Bible Quarterly* 32.4 (2004): 239-44. *Ebscohost*. Web. 2 April 2014.

Kawashima, Robert S. "The Jubilee, Every 49 or 50 Years?" *Vetus Testamentum* 53.1 (2003): 117-20. *Ebscohost*. Web. 3 May 2014.

Kim, Uriah Y. "Leviticus 25:1-24." *Interpretation* 65.4 (2011): 396-98. *Ebscohost*. Web. 2 April 2014.

Kim, Young Hye. "The Jubilee: Its Reckoning and Inception Day." *Vetus Testamentum* 60.1 (2010): 147-51. *Ebscohost*. Web. 2 April 2014.

Knohl, Israel. "The Priestly Torah versus the Holiness School: Sabbath and the Festivals." *Hebrew Union College Annual* 58 (1987): 65-117. *Ebscohost*. Web. 28 April 2014.

Ladd, George Eldon. "Eschatology." *The International Standard Bible Encyclopedia*. 1982 ed. Vol. 2. 130-43. Print.

Lamberty-Zielinski, H. "*miqrā'*." *Theological Dictionary of the Old Testament*. 2004 ed. Vol. 13. 132-34. Print.

Lemche, N. P. "The Hebrew Slave: Comments on the Slave Law, Ex 21:2-11." *Vetus Testamentum* 25.2 (1975): 129-44. *Ebscohost*. Web. 24 July 2014.

_____. "The Manumission of Slaves—the Fallow Year—the Sabbatical Year—the Jobel Year." *Vetus Testamentum* 26.1 (1976): 38-59. *Ebscohost*. Web. 2 April 2014.

Lewis, Jack P. "The Jewish Background of the Church." *Restoration Quarterly* 2.4 (1958): 154-63. *Ebscohost*. Web. 5 May 2014.

Lewy, Hildegard, and Julius Lewy. "The Origin of the Week and the Oldest West Asiatic Calendar." *Hebrew Union College Annual* 17 (1943): 1-152. *Ebscohost*. Web. 13 May 2014.

Lewy, Immanuel. "Our Sabbath: Origin and Significance." *Reconstructionist* 18.19 (1953): 21-25. *Ebscohost*. Web. 9 April 2014.

Lewy, Julius. "Origin and Signification of the Biblical Term 'Hebrew.'" *Hebrew Union College Annual* 28 (1957): 1-13. *Ebscohost*. Web. 24 July 2014.

Lincoln, Andrew T. "Sabbath, Rest, and Eschatology in the New Testament." *From Sabbath to Lord's Day: A Biblical, Historical, and Theological Investigation*. Ed. D. A. Carson. Grand Rapids: Academie Books, 1982. 197-220. Print.

Lohse, Eduard. "σάββατον." *Theological Dictionary of the New Testament*. 1971 ed. Vol. 7. 1-35. Print.

MacCarty, Skip. "The Seventh-Day Sabbath." *Perspectives on the Sabbath: Four Views*. Ed. Christopher John Donato. Nashville: B&H Academic, 2011. 9-72. Print.

Martin, Troy. "But Let Everyone Discern the Body of Christ (Colossians 2:17)." *Journal of Biblical Literature* 114.2 (1995): 249-55. *Ebscohost*. Web. 5 September 2014.

————, "Pagan and Judeo-Christian Time-Keeping Schemes in Gal 4.10 and Col 2.16." *New Testament Studies* 42.1 (1996): 105-19. Print.

McCann, J. C., Jr. "Sabbath." *The International Standard Bible Encyclopedia*. 1988 ed. Vol. 4. 247-52. Print.

McCullough, W. S. "A Re-Examination of Isaiah 56-66." *Journal of Biblical Literature* 67.1 (1948): 27-36. *Ebscohost*. Web. 5 July 2014.

McKay, Heather A. "From Evidence to Edifice: Four Fallacies about the Sabbath." *Text as Pretext: Essays in Honour of Robert Davidson*. Ed. Robert P. Carroll. Sheffield: JSOT Press, 1992. 179-99. Print. Journal for the Study of the Old Testament Supplement Series 138.

————, "New Moon or Sabbath?" *The Sabbath in Jewish and Christian Traditions*. Ed. Tamara C. Eskenazi, Daniel J. Harrington, and William H. Shea. New York: Crossroad, 1991. 12-27. Print.

Meek, Theophile James. "The Sabbath in the Old Testament: Its Origin and Development." *Journal of Biblical Literature* 33.3 (1914): 201-12. *Ebscohost*. Web. 9 April 2014.

Moltmann, Jürgen. "Sabbath: Finishing and Beginning." *Living Pulpit* 7.2 (1998): 4-5. *Ebscohost*. Web. 2 April 2014.

Morgenstern, Julian. "Two Compound Technical Terms in Biblical Hebrew." *Journal of Biblical Literature* 43.3-4 (1924): 311-20. *Ebscohost*. Web. 30 April 2014.

Nickelsburg, George W. E. "Eschatology (Early Jewish)." *Anchor Bible Dictionary*. 1992 ed. Vol. 2. 579-94. Print.

North, Robert. "*Yâd* in the Shemitta-Law." *Vetus Testamentum* 4.2 (1954): 196-99. *Ebscohost*. Web. 23 July 2014.

Novick, Tzvi. "Law and Loss: Response to Catastrophe in Numbers 15." *Harvard Theological Review* 101.1 (2008): 1-14. *Ebscohost*. Web. 6 June 2014.

Olson, Dennis T. "Sacred Time: The Sabbath and Christian Worship." *Sunday, Sabbath, and the Weekend: Managing Time in A Global Culture*. Ed. Edward O'Flaherty, Rodney L. Petersen, and Timothy A. Norton. Grand Rapids: Eerdmans, 2010. 43-66. Print.

Olyan, Saul M. "Exodus 31:12-17: The Sabbath according to H, or the Sabbath according to P and H?" *Journal of Biblical Literature* 124.2 (2005): 201-09. *Ebscohost*. Web. 4 February 2014.

Parsons, Mikeal C. "Mark 2:23-28." *Interpretation* 59.1 (2005): 57-60. *Ebscohost*. Web. 26 August 2014.

Petersen, David L. "Eschatology (Old Testament)." *Anchor Bible Dictionary*. 1992 ed. Vol. 2. 575-79. Print.

———, "The Formation of the Pentateuch." *Old Testament Interpretation: Past, Present, and Future: Essays in Honor of Gene M. Tucker*. Ed. James Luther Mays, David L. Petersen, and Kent Harold Richards. Nashville: Abingdon Press, 1995. 31-45. Print.

Phillips, Anthony. "The Case of the Woodgatherer Reconsidered." *Vetus Testamentum* 19.1 (1969): 125-28. *Ebscohost*. Web. 29 May 2014.

———, "The Laws of Slavery: Exodus 21:2-11." *Journal for the Study of the Old Testament* 30 (1984): 51-66. *Ebscohost*. Web. 24 July 2014.

Pipa, Joseph A. "The Christian Sabbath." *Perspectives on the Sabbath: Four Views*. Ed. Christopher John Donato. Nashville: B&H Academic, 2011. 119-71. Print.

Pruitt, Brad A. "The Sabbatical Year of Release: The Social Location and Practice of *Shemittah* in Deuteronomy 15:1-18." *Restoration Quarterly* 52.2 (2010): 81-92. *Ebscohost*. Web. 2 April 2014.

Rayburn, Robert G. "Should Christians Observe the Sabbath?" *Presbyterion* 10 (1984): 72-86. *Ebscohost*. Web. 2 April 2014.

Reymond, Robert L. "Lord's Day Observance: Man's Proper Response to the Fourth Commandment." *Presbyterion* 13.1 (1987): 7-23. *Ebscohost*. Web. 2 April 2014.

Robinson, Gnana. "The Prohibition of Strange Fire in Ancient Israel." *Vetus Testamentum* 28.3 (1978): 301-17. *Ebscohost*. Web. 7 April 2014.

Rooker, Mark F. "Dating Isaiah 40-66: What Does the Linguistic Evidence Say?" *Westminster Theological Journal* 58.2 (1996): 303-12. *Ebscohost*. Web. 5 July 2014.

Rowland, Chris. "A Summary of Sabbath Observance in Judaism at the Beginning of the Christian Era." *From Sabbath to Lord's Day: A Biblical, Historical, and Theological Investigation*. Ed. D. A. Carson. Grand Rapids: Academie Books, 1982. 43-55. Print.

Rowley, Harold H. "Moses and the Decalogue." *Bulletin of the John Rylands Library* 34.1 (1952): 81-118. Web. 11 May 2014. <https://www.

escholar.manchester.ac.uk/api/datastream?publicationPid=uk-ac-man-scw:1m2009&datastreamId=POST-PEER-REVIEW-PUBLISHERS-DOCUMENT.PDF>.

Schenker, Adrian. "The Biblical Legislation on the Release of Slaves: The Road from Exodus to Leviticus." *Journal for the Study of the Old Testament* 78 (1998): 23-41. *Ebscohost*. Web. 21 July 2014.

Shead, Andrew G. "An Old Testament Theology of the Sabbath Year and Jubilee." *Reformed Theological Review* 61.1 (2002): 19-33. *Ebscohost*. Web. 3 May 2014.

Sherman, Robert. "Reclaimed by Sabbath Rest." *Interpretation* 59.1 (2005): 38-50. *Ebscohost*. Web. 2 April 2014.

Smith, Morton. "Jewish Religious Life in the Persian Period." *The Cambridge History of Judaism*. Ed. W. D. Davies and Louis Finkelstein. Vol. 1. Cambridge: Cambridge University Press, 1984. 219-78. Print.

Stackert, Jeffrey. "The Sabbath of the Land in the Holiness Legislation: Combining Priestly and Non-Priestly Perspectives." *Catholic Biblical Quarterly* 73.2 (2011): 239-50. *Ebscohost*. Web. 21 July 2014.

Stolz, F. "שבת." *Theological Lexicon of the Old Testament*. 1997 ed. Vol. 3. 1297-1302. Print.

Tsevat, Matitiahu. "Alalakhiana." *Hebrew Union College Annual* 29 (1958): 109-34. *Ebscohost*. Web. 8 August 2014.

Tuell, Steven S. "Genesis 2:1-3." *Interpretation* 59.1 (2005): 51-53. *Ebscohost*. Web. 26 August 2014.

Unger, Merrill F. "The Significance of the Sabbath." *Bibliotheca Sacra* 123.489 (1966): 53-59. *Ebscohost*. Web. 22 May 2014.

Van Henten, J. W. "Angel II ἄγγελος." *Dictionary of Deities and Demons in the Bible*. 2nd ed. Ed. Karel van der Toorn, Bob Becking, and Pieter W. van der Horst. Leiden: Brill, 1999. 50-53. Print.

Van Seters, John. "The Law of the Hebrew Slave." *Zeitschrift für die alttestamentliche Wissenschaft* 108.4 (1996): 534-46. *Ebscohost*. Web. 24 July 2014.

———, "Law of the Hebrew Slave: A Continuing Debate." *Zeitschrift für die alttestamentliche Wissenschaft* 119.2 (2007): 169-83. *Ebscohost*. Web. 24 July 2014.

Wassen, Cecilia. "Angels in the Dead Sea Scrolls." *Angels: The Concept of Celestial Beings—Origins, Development and Reception*. Ed. Friedrich V. Reiterer, Tobias Nicklas, and Karin Schöpflin. Berlin: Walter de Gruyter, 2007. 499-523. Print. Deuterocanonical and Cognate Literature.

Waterman, G. H. "Sabbath." *Zondervan Pictorial Encyclopedia of the Bible*. 1976 ed. Vol. 5. 181-89. Print.

Weingreen, Jacob. "The Case of the Woodgatherer (Numbers XV 32-36)." *Vetus Testamentum* 16.3 (1966): 361-64. *Ebscohost*. Web. 27 May 2014.

Weiss, von Herold. "Paul and the Judging of Days." *Zeitschrift für die neutestamentliche Wissenschaft und die Kunde der älteren Kirche* 86.3-4 (1995): 137-53. *Ebscohost.* Web. 12 September 2014.

Wenham, Gordon J. "Pondering the Pentateuch: The Search for a New Paradigm." *The Face of Old Testament Studies: A Survey of Contemporary Approaches.* Ed. David W. Baker and Bill T. Arnold. Grand Rapids: Baker, 1999. 116-44. Print.

————, "The Priority of P." *Vetus Testamentum* 49.2 (1999): 240-58. *Ebscohost.* Web. 25 June 2014.

Wolff, Hans Walter. "The Day of Rest in the Old Testament." *Concordia Theological Monthly* 43.8 (1972): 498-506. *Ebscohost.* Web. 22 May 2014.

Wright, Christopher J. H. "What Happened Every Seven Years in Israel? Old Testament Sabbatical Institutions for Land, Debts and Slaves, Part I." *Evangelical Quarterly* 56.3 (1984): 129-38. Web. 22 July 2014. <http://www.biblicalstudies.org.uk/pdf/eq/1984-3_wright.pdf >.

————, "What Happened Every Seven Years in Israel? Old Testament Sabbatical Institutions for Land, Debts and Slaves, Part II." *Evangelical Quarterly* 56.4 (1984): 193-201. Web. 22 July 2014. <http://www.biblicalstudies.org.uk/pdf/eq/1984-4_wright.pdf>.

Wright, D. P., and J. Milgrom. "עָצַר." *Theological Dictionary of the Old Testament.* 2001 ed. Vol. 11. 310-15. Print.

Zerubavel, Eviatar. "The Jewish Week: Its Origin and Essence." *Reconstructionist* 50.8 (1985): 16-20. *Ebscohost.* Web. 8 May 2014.

Online Sources

100% Cotton Made in India. Dir. Inge Altemeier. Altemeier & Hornung Filmproduktion, 2003. *YouTube.* Web. 18 October 2013. <http://www.youtube.com/watch?v=ol9LhGQJQ_w>.

Abid, Rubab. "The Myth of India's 'GM Genocide': Genetically Modified Cotton Blamed for Wave of Farmer Suicides." *National Post.* 26 January 2013. Web. 17 October 2013. <http://news.nationalpost.com/2013/01/26/the-myth-of-indias-gm-genocide-genetically-modified-cotton-blamed-for-wave-of-farmer-suicides/>.

Center for Human Rights and Global Justice. *Every Thirty Minutes: Farmer Suicides, Human Rights, and the Agrarian Crisis in India.* New York: NYU School of Law, 2011. Web. 18 October 2013. <http://chrgj.org/wp-content/uploads/2012/10/Farmer-Suicides.pdf>.

Farmers in India Commit Suicide over GM Cotton; Bt Cotton gets 'Punjab-ed' in India. By Dale Willis. Food Offensive: From the Front Lines of Our Food Supply. 19 March 2012. *YouTube.* Web. 18 October 2013. <http://www.youtube.com/watch?v=AM7_34Mi2no>.

Greenhouse, Steven. "Report Cites Forced Labor in Malaysia's Electronics Industry." *The New York Times.* 17 September 2014. Web. 18 September 2014. <http://www.nytimes.com/2014/09/17/business/international/report-cites-forced-labor-in-malaysia.html?_r=0>.

Gucciardi, Anthony. "Monsanto's GMO Seeds Contributing to Farmer Suicides Every 30 Minutes." *Infowars.com.* 4 April 2012. Web. 16 October 2013. <http://www.infowars.com/monsantos-gmo-seeds-contributing-to-farmer-suicides-every-30-minutes/>.

Malone, Andrew. "The GM Genocide: Thousands of Indian Farmers are Committing Suicide after Using Genetically Modified Crops." *Mail Online.* 3 November 2008. Web. 17 October 2013. <http://www.dailymail.co.uk/news/article-1082559/The-GM-genocide-Thousands-Indian-farmers-committing-suicide-using-genetically-modified-crops.html>.

Pain, Paromita. "Battling India's Monsanto Protection Act, Farmers Demand End to GMO." *Occupy.com.* 22 August 2013. Web. 16 October 2013. <http://www.truth-out.org/news/item/18337-battling-indias-monsanto-protection-act-farmers-demand-end-to-gmo>.

Pentland, William. "Every 30 Minutes an Indian Farmer Commits Suicide, Biotech is Not to Blame." *Forbes.com.* 18 May 2011. Web. 16 October 2013. <http://www.forbes.com/sites/williampentland/2011/05/18/every-30-minutes-an-indian-farmer-commits-suicide-biotech-is-not-to-blame/>.

Peterson, Eugene H. "The Pastor's Sabbath." *Leadership Journal.* 19 May 2004. Web. 29 July 2014. <http://www.christianitytoday.com/le/topics/soul/sabbath/lclead04-2.html>.

Sherman, Daniel. *PastorBurnout.com.* <www.pastorburnout.com>.